Across the waters of ⸻
Lord Malachite woke in his bachelor drey in one of
the Scots pines on Tanglewood Knoll. He looked
over to the next tree where Lord Silica had a similar
establishment, and then across the sunlit glade to
where Lord Obsidian lived, also on his own.

What are we doing here? he thought, not for the
first time. Two, maybe even three, winters have
passed since we set up that Power Square to protect
us from the plague of the Grey Death. We'll all die
here forgotten in this foreign wood unless we get out
there and do something . . .

Malachite was half watching an ichneumon fly
probing through the pine bark with the long spike
under her tail, seeking wood-boring grubs in which
to lay her eggs. The other half of his mind, preoccupied with his ambition, ranged across New
America to the Oval Drey at Woburn where the
leader of all the Silver Squirrels lived and ruled by
edict. One day I will be the Great Lord Silver, he
was thinking. One day!

Michael Tod was born in 1937 in Dorset, where this story is set. He lived near Weymouth until his family moved to a hill farm in Wales when he was eleven. His childhood experiences on the Dorset coast and in the Welsh mountains have given him a deep love and knowledge of wild creatures and the countryside, which is reflected in his poetry and fiction and inspired *The Woodstock Saga*. Married, with three children and three grandchildren, he still lives, works and walks in his beloved Welsh hills, but visits his old haunts in Dorset whenever he can.

By the same author

The Silver Tide
The Second Wave

The Golden Flight

MICHAEL TOD

ORION

An Orion paperback
First published in Great Britain
by Orion in 1995
This paperback edition published in 1996
by Orion Books Ltd,
Orion House, 5 Upper St Martin's Lane,
London WC2H 9EA

Text copyright © Michael Tod 1995
Maps copyright © Orion Books Ltd 1995

A CIP catalogue record for this book
is available from the British Library.

ISBN: 0 75280 618 1

Printed and bound in Great Britain by
Clays Ltd, St Ives plc

To those who care enough to teach

Maps

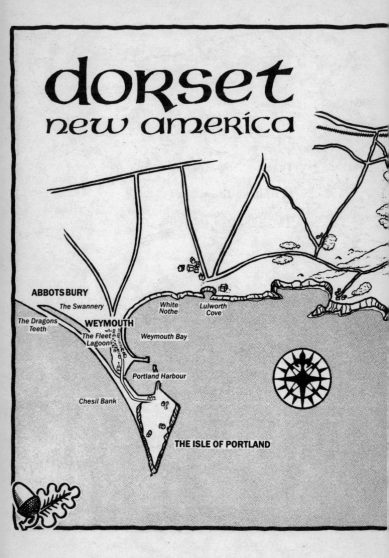

dorset
new america

ABBOTS BURY

The Swannery

White Nothe

Lulworth Cove

The Dragons Teeth

WEYMOUTH

The Fleet Lagoon

Weymouth Bay

Portland Harbour

Chesil Bank

THE ISLE OF PORTLAND

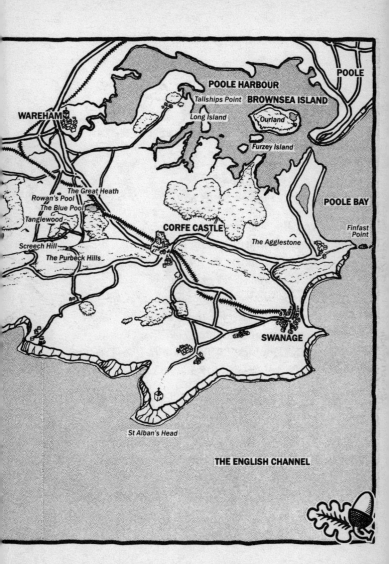

POOLE

POOLE HARBOUR

BROWNSEA ISLAND

Tallships Point

Long Island

Ourland

WAREHAM

Furzey Island

POOLE BAY

The Great Heath

Rowan's Pool

The Blue Pool

Tanglewood

CORFE CASTLE

Finfast Point

The Agglestone

Screech Hill

The Purbeck Hills

SWANAGE

St Alban's Head

THE ENGLISH CHANNEL

Characters

RED SQUIRRELS OF OURLAND

Marguerite the Seeker
Burdock and *Oak*, her daughter and son
Just Poplar the Leader; his life-mate *Rush* the Kind
Her son, *Chip* Who Seeks Love
Dandelion the Story-teller; her life-mate *Alder*
Larch the Curious; his life-mate *Clover* the Tagger
Their son *Elm* and daughter *Trefoil*
Chestnut the Doubter; his life-mate *Heather* Treetops
Tamarisk Greatleap; his life-mate *Tansy* Stoutheart

Ex-Kingz-Mate *Thizle*
The ex-princesses, *Cowzlip* and *Voxglove* the Carers
Their brother, ex-prince *Fir*

Walnut (Old Wally) a long-dead squirrel who made
prophecies
Caterpillar an ex-zervant
Sycamore, a young red squirrel

RED SQUIRRELS ON THE MAINLAND

Rowan the Bold; his life-mate *Meadowsweet* Rowan's Love
Their daughter *Bluebell*
Spindle the Helpful; his life-mate *Wood Anemone* the Able (was
Woodlouse)
Their twin daughters *Rosebay* and *Willowherb*

GREY SQUIRRELS ON THE MAINLAND

Hickory
Sitka
Sumac; his life-mate *Tumbleweed*

THE THREE GREY LORDS

Lord *Malachite*
Lord *Obsidian*
Lord *Silica*

The Great Lord Silvers – *Redwood* and *Monterey*
Monterey's namesake, a young grey squirrel
Many Colonisers under training

OTHERS

The Dolphins, *Malin* and *Lundy*
Their son *Finisterre*
Acorn and *Primrose*, the mythical first squirrels in the world
Swans from Abbotsbury Swannery

Chapter 1

———

March 1964 roared in upon Dorset.

The great sweep of the Chesil Bank in Dorset was taking the full force of the south-westerly gale as a deep depression drove in from the Atlantic. For over twenty miles pebbles snarled and ground as the heavy seas rushed in, each wave tumbling over the previous one in its haste. The churning action rounded the stones and moved them ever eastwards, sorting the pebbles by size as they trundled along. To the west the shingle was pea-sized, whereas at the aptly named Deadman's Bay at the Portland end of the beach it ranged in size from that of a potato to that of a giant swede.

By nightfall the waves were breaking over the crest of the Bank and rushing down the far side, tearing out the mats of sea-campion that grew on the landward slope above the more sheltered waters of the Fleet Lagoon.

The usually smooth surface of the Fleet was choppy and debris-laden as gusts of wind carried plastic bottles, fishing-net corks, small pieces of driftwood and dead seaweed from the top of the Chesil Bank and tossed them all into the lagoon behind.

Where Mute swans had nested on the mainland side of

the Fleet for over six hundred years, a flock now huddled on their nest sites, heads tucked under their wings to keep dust and flying reeds from their eyes.

There was no rain, but even at that distance, the air was misted with a fine salt spray which formed little pools on the swans' feathers and trickled in tiny rivulets to the ground.

The most seaward pair of the Dragon's Teeth, a double line of concrete tank-stops that had straddled the beach since the fear of invasion in 1939, were undermined by the waves and drawn down into the depths by the suction of the undertow. The deep rolling action of the waves disturbed the wrecks that lay off that treacherous coast, and pieces of jagged iron from landing craft and tramp steamers, together with waterlogged timbers from emigrant ships and Armada galleons were thrown up the beach and dragged down again, artefacts and treasures spilling across the seabed.

Further along the coast, the massive bulk of Portland stood firm against this storm as it had for ten thousand years and a thousand similar storms, protecting the deep waters of Weymouth Bay to the east.

Even so, the cliffs from White Nothe to Saint Alban's Head were being pounded and eroded by the giant waves gnawing at their feet, bringing down cascades of chalky rock. Only at Lulworth Cove, where the narrow entrance excluded all but an occasional wave, was there calmer water. Here a few waves rolled in and exhausted themselves in the enclosed bay; the swoosh as each ran gently up the beach being drowned by the howling of the gale overhead.

The wind tore at the cliffs surrounding the cove, probing into every nook and cranny as though seeking out seabirds to toss through the air, but these birds, sensing an impending storm, had already flown inland.

Frustrated, the wind raced over the land, shaking and felling great oak trees and working loose the tiles and thatch on the cottages of the humans.

At the Tanglewood Knoll on the Great Heath, the wind found no new trees to topple. Another such storm some fifteen years before had felled all those that were not well-rooted or were past their prime. The tangled trunks and branches on the ground below the standing pines gave the wood its name and protected it from the forays of gun-bearing humans.

In one of these pines, three elderly grey squirrels huddled together in a drey, feeling the wind rock the tree and expecting any minute that the drey itself would be blown out of the fork, and the twigs and mossy lining scattered over the wood. They feared that they too might be flung to the ground but each tried to hide his fears from the others.

Further to the east near the Blue Pool, now a wind-whipped mass of foam and bubbles, seven red squirrels had just had their drey torn to pieces around them. Shaken and breathless they were hurrying along the ground to seek shelter in a hollow tree, known to them as the Warren Ash. The wind fluffed up their tails and fur, and the stronger gusts bowled them over on the shifting, rustling mass of pine needles forming the forest floor.

Even further to the east, the wind picked up speed as it crossed the frothing waters of Poole Harbour to throw itself at the screen of trees that encircled the island of Brownsea;

trees that surrounded and protected the meadows and the woodlands at the island's centre. One violent gust caught a giant pine growing just behind the southern shore and snapped its trunk some six feet above the ground, the top bounding and rolling across the trackway behind, to lodge in the mass of romping rhododendron bushes.

This final act of vandalism seemed to satisfy the wind. As darkness fell, the force slackened and the stars, pricking through the blackness above the island, looked down on a ravaged landscape.

A moon later, in the mild spring sunshine Marguerite, a mature red squirrel, sat on top of The Wall. Not a wall – The Wall.

This brick-built structure was in the centre of Ourland, a beautiful island of woodland, meadows and heath set in the now placid waters of Poole Harbour. The Wall had once formed the back of a range of glass-houses which had provided grapes, peaches and other exotic fruit to the inhabitants of the Castle at the island's eastern end. After many years of neglect, all that remained of the hot houses and the vegetable garden was The Wall.

It was about twice the height of a man and ran parallel to a track which had recently been cleared of undergrowth.

Marguerite had climbed the weathered brickwork, her claws finding holds in the crumbling mortar between the bricks. In these crevices moss grew, and from the top of The Wall, gossamer spiders' webs reached out to nearby bushes.

She sat listening to the young squirrels playing at the other end of The Wall. From where she was she could not

OURLAND
BROWNSEA ISLAND

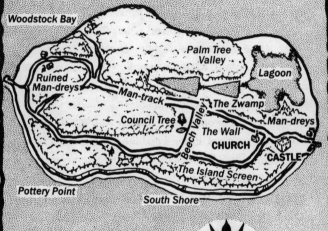

Woodstock Bay

Palm Tree Valley

Lagoon

Ruined Man-dreys

Man-track

The Zwamp

Man-dreys

Council Tree

Beech Valley

The Wall

CHURCH

CASTLE

The Island Screen

Pottery Point

South Shore

Furzey Island

count them, but by the sound of their playful chatter there were "lots". In fact, she realised there were lots of young squirrels all over the island.

Now that the Scourge of Ourland, the pine marten, was dead, there were no predators to fear, and the happy squirrels were following their Sun-inspired desires, mating and producing many healthy young dreylings. Something about all this had been making Marguerite feel slightly uneasy but she had not yet put a paw on the problem. She moved along the top of the wall to watch the game.

Having lived on the Mainland when she was a youngster, this island game was new to her. The rules seemed fairly simple. The young squirrels would scurry about on the ground while one climbed the wall and began a chant, at which all the others froze wherever they were. When the chant was complete, the squirrel on the wall selected a victim by calling their name and then tried to leap down onto him or her. No squirrel could move until a name had been called. If the leaping squirrel caught the named one, it could nip it with its teeth, but if it missed, the triumphant victim climbed the wall and took over as Leaper.

Marguerite watched for a while, listening to the chant with interest. It had the five, seven, five, sound pattern of a Kernel of Truth, yet the words did not make sense – perhaps she was mis-hearing them. Kernels should always make their meaning clear at once. There was even one which said:

A Kernel's message
Should be wrapped in gossamer
Clever wraps obscure.

She moved closer, but her presence disturbed the youngsters, who held her in some awe. The game stopped, leaving the young squirrels sitting about uncomfortably.

"I'm sorry," Marguerite called down. "I didn't want to spoil your fun, I was just trying to hear what you were saying. How does that chant go?"

The current "Leaper", who she recognised as Dandelion's youngest daughter, turned to her and replied,

> *I honour birch-bark,*
> *The Island Screen. Flies stinging –*
> *A piece of the sun.*

"What does it mean?" Marguerite asked, intrigued.

"I don't know," the youngster replied. "It's what we always say – does it have to mean anything? It's just a game."

Another dreyling, Elm, Larch's son, called up from the ground, "When you get caught and nipped, it's like a fly's sting."

"Uz father wuz ztung by a wazp onze," another youngster volunteered, his accent showing that his father must be one of the original islanders. "Nazdy, him zaid it wuz. Him taught uz to ztay away from yellow thingz that flyz."

No other comments were offered and Marguerite thanked them politely and as she went back along The Wall, she heard the game restart.

> *I honour birch-bark . . .*

7

What could it mean, she wondered.

She had recently abandoned her attempts to make sense of humans' name shapes. **A** for Acorn was fine, and she had always used **X** as her special mark, so **X** must be for Marguerite; but after this she could get no further. Here was a new challenge!

I honour birch-bark
The Island Screen. Flies stinging –
A piece of the sun.

She repeated it several times to herself. The Island Screen was the name that the squirrels called the ring of trees which surrounded the open areas and the woodland, protecting them from the gales and the storms, but the Screen was mostly pine with only a few birches. Why should *their* bark be especially mentioned?

She climbed down The Wall, and wandered aimlessly towards the meadows to the south. Much overgrown from many years of neglect, the meadows were host to a variety of fungi in the autumn and a few grew right through from spring. Even now there were rings of small buff-coloured mushroom-shapes pushing up through the rank grass. Marguerite had often wondered why this kind grew in rings and why some squirrels called other kinds, toad's stools. Although Chestnut the Doubter wouldn't call them that. *He'd* never seen a toad sitting on one.

She nibbled cautiously at the edge of a small one, it was not unpleasant though the cap was quite tough. It would probably store well for winter food, she thought. One had to be very careful with tasting, especially fungi, she knew that some could be deadly poisonous and should be avoided.

> *Curiosity*
> *Drives discovery. Beware –*
> *Daring fools may die.*

Another Kernel of Truth. Her mind went back to the chant. If the *chant* was a Kernel, she was thinking, it should not be obscure – *Clever wraps obscure*. One could equally say *Clumsy wraps obscure*. Kernels should be clear and easy to understand!

Nearing the Zwamp, she decided to call on Ex-Kingz-Mate, Thizle, who had lived there alone since the deposed King had been killed and eaten by the pine marten. She knew many of the old island customs.

Thizle was pleased to see her and welcomed her in the island dialect, "Greetingz to yew, Marguerite-Friend. What newz do yew have fur uz? Uz do mizz the Pozt zquirrelz."

Marguerite could just recall the smart Royal Post Squirrels who used to sit on their posts at Dawn, High-sun and Dusk waiting for messages to be given to them. These they would relay faithfully and accurately to other squirrels all over the island. How proud they had been and how accurately they had reported; but with the abolition of the Monarchy, the Post Squirrels' role had also disappeared.

Marguerite sat with the old squirrel in the sunshine outside her drey and told her of the many things that were happening on the island. How, with so many squirrels, it was no longer possible for all of them to put their views at

Council so attendance was falling. There was talk of having to have two or even more Councils covering different parts of the island.

"Uz can't zay uz'z happy about that," the old Ex-Kingz-Mate told Marguerite. "Yew can get each lot quarrelling with the otherz, and Zun-knowz where yew endz up then.

"Uz do mizz the Old Dayz – uz loved the ceremoneez. There wuz Vinding the Verzd Veather – the Monarch'z Moon Muzhroomz – Greeting the Geeze – uz loved all of thoze."

Marguerite smiled at her, then asked about the Birch-bark Kernel.

"That'z one of old Wally'z prophezeez," she was told. "Wally uzed to live near The Wall, before uz wuz born. Wally'z real name wuz Walnut, and many zquirrelz thought he wuz not quite right in the head. He wuz alwayz coming out with zum prophezy or other. Rubbizh, mozt of it."

"Do you know what the Birch-bark one means?" Marguerite asked again.

Thizle recited it.

> Hie honourz birch-bark
> The i'land'z zcreen. Fliez ztinging –
> The pieze of the zun.

Marguerite noted that Thizle had said *Hie* instead of *I* or *Uz*, and had used *The piece* instead of *A piece*.

"Isn't it *A piece*?" she asked.

"It used to be *The* pieze but uz mate, King Willow, Zun rezd hiz bonez, changed it. He zaid that a fly'z zting iz hot like a pieze of the zun, zo it zhould be *A pieze*. It made more zenze, he zaid."

Marguerite still could not make of sense of it and so changed the subject. "Do you think this fine weather will last?" she asked.

Chapter 2

Chip took the sloe that Caterpillar handed him. It was warm from the heat generated inside the leaf pile, and it smelled over-ripe and rotten.

"Try it, it won't hurt yew," Caterpillar told him.

Chip hesitated. He knew that Marguerite would not approve, and that eating the ruddled sloes was only permitted to the three ex-zervantz who had successfully pleaded to the Council that they would be ill if they did not have one regularly.

"Are yew frit?" asked Caterpillar.

"Of course not," said Chip, looking about him before biting into the wrinkled black skin. The taste was not unpleasant and he swallowed the mouthful, feeling a warm sensation as it passed down into his stomach. He took another bite.

Caterpillar was already eating his third when Chip's legs tangled with each other and he fell forwards onto the moist warm leaves.

Word passed round the island as quickly as the scent of gorse on a summer's day. Chip, Marguerite's protégé, had been found ruddled at the leaf pile and had been summoned to appear before the Council. It would have to be a down-tag for him. Every squirrel knew the rule about the ruddled sloes. Would Marguerite stand by him?

The Island Council met in the tree above the pond in Beech Valley to hear the case against Chip. Though recently few squirrels had been attending meetings, so many squirrels were present that day that some had to sit in the next tree, straining their ears to hear the proceedings above the gentle rustle of the wind in the beech-leaves.

Clover the Tagger was in charge. Chip, his head thumping, sat, tail low, on the branch near her. Marguerite was at his side.

"Chip Who Seeks Love," Clover began sternly, quoting the tag Chip had earned the previous year. "It has been reported that you have been eating ruddled sloes, although you know this to be forbidden. Is this true?"

Chip looked at Marguerite, who nodded her head. "Yes," he replied, his tail drooping even lower.

"Why did you do this, when you knew it to be wrong?" Clover asked.

Chip looked around at the mass of squirrels but could not see Caterpillar. "Just did," he replied sullenly.

Clover waited, but Chip rubbed his paws together nervously and said nothing more.

"Does any squirrel have anything to say before I consider a new tag for Chip?" Clover asked.

Marguerite stepped forward and quoted the Understanding Kernel:

If you could know all
Then you could understand all
Then you'd forgive all.

Clover looked at her old friend and recalled how the year before they had stood against one another for the position of "Tagger of Ourland" and knew that Marguerite was doing her best for Chip. However if *he* would not explain his actions, there was no other choice but to down-tag him.

Clover waited, looking expectantly at Chip. He sat very still until she ordered him to leave the Council whilst they discussed his action. He moved to a tree out of ear-twitch.

There was little discussion. The offence was clear, the offender had admitted it, and had been given the opportunity to tell his story. As it said in the Kernel:

Squirrels have the right
To explain their own actions,
Fully – in silence.

Called back, he was given the tag "the Ruddled", and, feeling ashamed of himself, Chip the Ruddled left in disgrace, his tail trailing.

As for Caterpillar, he seemed to have important business that kept him on the far side of the island for several weeks!

Across the waters of the harbour, on the Mainland, Lord Malachite woke in his bachelor drey in one of the Scots pines on Tanglewood Knoll. He looked over to the next tree where Lord Silica had a similar establishment, and then across the sunlit glade to where Lord Obsidian lived, also on his own.

What are we doing here? he thought, not for the first time. Two, maybe even three, winters have passed since we set up that Power Square to protect us from the plague of the Grey Death. We'll all die here forgotten in this foreign wood unless we get out there and do something.

The thought disturbed him and he recalled his ambition.

As with all the male grey squirrels in New America, he had cherished the idea of becoming the Great Lord Silver. Like his two companions, he had earned the first rank of Lord through his ruthless treatment of the native Reds. Then the Grey Death came, forcing the three of them to flee and hide here on this knoll in the Great Heath. Humans never came into this wood, the storm-felled tree trunks on the knoll having made an effective barrier.

"Lord Silica," he called across to the next tree, "are you awake?"

"I am now, damn you," a voice growled from the next drey. "What is it?"

Taken aback by the gruffness of the response, Lord Malachite did not answer, but came fully out into the sunshine and sat on the branch listening to the soft "Coo – coo, coo-coo" of a wood pigeon on the other side of the wood.

"What is it you want?" Lord Silica had emerged from his drey and was looking across at Lord Malachite.

"I was just wondering if we were going to pass the rest of our lives here, that's all. I'm bored and was wondering if the Grey Death has gone yet?"

A rustling of pine needles betrayed the approach of Lord Obsidian. "What are you two plotting?" he asked.

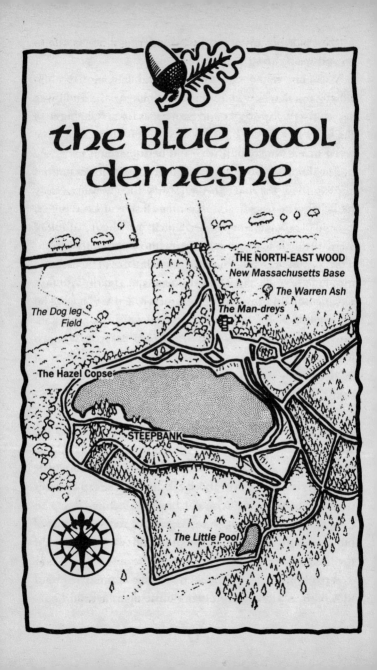

the Blue pool demesne

THE NORTH-EAST WOOD
New Massachusetts Base

The Warren Ash

The Dog leg Field

The Man-dreys

The Hazel Copse

STEEPBANK

The Little Pool

"Not plotting anything. Just wondering if it was safe to go and see if the Grey Death has gone."

Malachite noted that Obsidian was looking older. So was Silica. Paunchy, too; the living here on the knoll was easy, with plenty of nuts and pine cones for just the three of them.

"If we ever mean to leave, we'd better make it soon," he said. "Why don't we go as far as that Blue Pool place; see if any squirrels survived there. If they did, they probably can't pass the plague on to us after all this time."

"We'll go tomorrow," said Silica, "or maybe the day after." He yawned and went back into his drey.

Malachite was half watching an ichneumon fly probing through the pine bark with the long spike under her tail, seeking wood-boring grubs in which to lay her eggs. The other half of his mind, preoccupied with his ambition, ranged across New America to the Oval Drey at Woburn where the leader of all the Silver Squirrels lived and ruled by edict. One day I will be the Great Lord Silver, he was thinking. One day!

Near the Blue Pool, in the woodland that the Greys called New Massachusetts, but was known to the native Reds by the more prosaic name of the North-east Wood, a middle-aged red squirrel known as Rowan the Bold was preparing the last teaching session for the batch of Greys that had formed his Early Spring class. These had arrived soon after the storm had blown itself out and, finding most of the old dreys had been torn down, eagerly began building new dreys to replace them. Rowan had noted with interest that they built to a new design, more basic than the traditional "family" ones. Their new dreys had room only for a single squirrel, though two Reds, being smaller, might just have been able to share. The Greys had a new name for them too – dreytels.

Rowan was joined by his life-mate Meadowsweet, their daughter Bluebell, and the ex-zervantz Spindle and Wood Anemone together with their twin daughters, Rosebay and Willowherb.

After greeting one another, Rowan asked Spindle if he had seen Hickory and Sitka.

"Them'z probably zeeing that the coloniztz have left the dreytelz tidy; them'll be along here zoon." Spindle replied, his accent giving away his island origin.

Hickory and Sitka had been the leaders of the Greys who had been misled by the Temple Master the year before. After losing the battle at the Agglestone Rock, they had stayed here with Rowan and his party, helping to teach new batches of colonists the ways of the natives, as directed by their leader, the current Great Lord Silver, from his base at Woburn.

The Early Spring class had learned well and were now moving on to colonise lands to the far west, though one pair, Sumac and Tumbleweed, had decided to make their home on Screech Hill across the Great Heath to the south-west.

The session that Rowan had prepared for this last teaching day was mostly revision of the more important Kernels of Truth and, by High-sun he could sense that the Greys were all eager to leave and put some of these teachings into practice. He dismissed the class and the Reds brushed whiskers with their ex-pupils and watched the new colonists troop excitedly off across the Dogleg Field, heading westwards.

"Do you know when the next batch is due in?" Rowan asked Hickory.

"I would think that they'll be here with the first showing of the New Moon," he replied.

Chapter 3

—

Sumac, with his mate Tumbleweed, had been among the new graduates when they had crossed the Dogleg Field and the humans' roadway. On the far side of that they had waved farewell to their class-mates. The mass of Greys had headed west, seeking lands to colonise.

Some of the ideas these friendly Reds had introduced him to were very different to the traditional concepts of the Greys. Guardianship, for instance; being responsible for an area instead of owning and defending it against all comers. Then there was this idea of Life-mating. He looked at Tumbleweed as she sat watching the others going out of sight. Did he really want to spend his whole life with her, rather than "play the wood" as Grey males had tradition-ally done? Did she share his views on all the things they had been taught?

Sumac had decided that they would not travel with the others but would see if he could find a vacant territory to look after on Screech Hill which he could see forming a hump on the skyline to the south-west. Supposing that any Greys he encountered were not friendly or still practised the old ways?

"Wait here," he told Tumbleweed, "I need to go back and ask Rowan something. I won't be long." He checked that there were none of the humans' travelling boxes coming along the roadway from either direction, and then scurried across.

The horses that lived in the Dogleg Field were down at the far end of the field and did not see him as he hopped across it, avoiding the piles of dung that littered the cropped grass, sun, rain and beetles breaking each down to return the borrowed nourishment to the soil below. Soon he was with Rowan.

"Hello, Sumac-Friend," Rowan greeted his star pupil. "I thought you had left."

"I had, but there is something that I needed to ask you."

Rowan raised an eyebrow and waited.

"It's about the Sun. I've listened to all you taught us and everything makes sense to me, but most of the other Greys were not so convinced. How can I tell whether or not any Grey I meet is a true believer?"

"As you are obviously a Sun-squirrel, I will let you into a secret." Rowan replied. "What does *this* mean to you?"

He scratched ⟨✕ in the dirt where they were sitting.

"It looks like a fish to me," said Sumac.

"Right," said Rowan. "That's what it is. Marguerite, my sister, learned the shape from some dolphins – you remember I told you about them. We Sun-squirrels use it to let others know what we are."

"But what has a fish got to do with being a Sun-squirrel?"

"Nothing, that's why we use it. If we used a symbol like this, ☀, it would be easy to guess its meaning. So, if you are not sure of a squirrel's beliefs just idly make the fish mark and any Sun-squirrel will recognise it and identify himself."

"Thank you my friend."

The red and the grey squirrels brushed whiskers.

"The Sun be with you."

"And with you."

Sumac was about to hurry back to Tumbleweed when he remembered a Kernel that Meadowsweet had taught him.

> *Squirrels do not live*
> *By nuts alone. Take time off*
> *To seek out beauty.*

He changed his direction and set off to circle the Blue Pool for one last time, relishing the bright azure colour of its still waters where it lay deep among the green of the pines and the banks of purple rhododendron flowers, flamboyant against their glossy dark leaves.

Tumbleweed was waiting impatiently. "Where in the Sunless-pit have you been?" she snapped.

Sumac decided that it was not the right time for him to explain about ⋖✕ symbols and Sun-squirrels.

Larch the Curious looked at the tree that had lost its top in the Great Storm. The splintered trunk was silhouetted against the dawn sky and he thought it looked like a giant squirrel; two spikes of torn wood fibres forming its tufted ears.

He ran up the scaly bark and bit at some of the exposed wood, then came down for another look. It was even more like a squirrel now, only the nose was wrong. He went up again and gnawed at that area. By the time the sun was well up, his teeth and jaws were aching from his efforts and he climbed an unbroken tree to rest. It was too early in the year for the boatloads of human visitors to arrive, but he always enjoyed this daytime snooze in the high branches. He wished that his life-mate Clover would join him, but knew that she was off somewhere with the two ex-princesses, Cowzlip and Voxglove.

Clover had told him that she had been planning a special kind of drey with them. Cowzlip and Voxglove had taken over her role as Carer and had suggested that they ought to have another drey near their own for sick squirrels to use. A further drey was to hold a selection of healing herbs.

This was all very well, thought Larch, but with Clover doing her best as Tagger for the increasing population of the island *and* this involvement with the Carers, she had little time to spend with him.

Larch admitted to himself that he was bored. Making that broken tree look like a squirrel had been fun; it had certainly made the time pass more quickly.

He was waking from a lazy afternoon's dozing when his son and daughter joined him.

"Greetings, Larch-Pa," they said together and he greeted them in return.

"Come and look at this," he said, leading them to where they could see the shape of a squirrel's head against the sky.

"That's great, Larch-Pa," Elm said, glancing at his sister and trying to keep a straight face, "but its forepaws are wrong."

"I haven't done anything to those," Larch said.

"It looks as if it's holding a Woodstock," said Trefoil. "With a bit of careful shaping it would scare off any pine marten."

Larch looked round apprehensively. It was only the year before that the pine marten which had terrorised the island squirrels had been killed. Sun, save us from any more, he thought.

Trefoil and Elm were already up the broken tree biting at the flaking bark and trimming off some of the dead twigs and small branches which were sticking out.

"A bit more off that one," Larch called up to Elm.

Chapter 4

Marguerite was concerned about Chip. Since he had come to Ourland he had outgrown a lot of the shyness which had, without doubt been caused by his fear of his father, the dreadful Crag. The young squirrel, for whom she had a special affection, had proved to be very clever, but since he had been down-tagged, little had been seen of him. She asked other squirrels if they knew where Chip was and one told her that he was twisting rushes together down near the Zwamp. It was here that she found him, engrossed with something that he had made and, so as not to frighten him, she called, "Chip, it's me," as she approached.

The young squirrel looked up, apparently pleased to see her, and held out the thing he had made. "Look at this," he said proudly.

Marguerite reached out and took the square of woven rushes from his paws. Across the hollow of the square were single pithy stems of reedmace and on each were threaded several rings of cherry bark. Marguerite had often seen hollow reddish-brown tubes of bark on the ground beneath wild cherry trees where the tough outer coverings of fallen twigs and small branches had been slower to rot than the softer wood inside. Chip had evidently bitten one of these tubes into rings. She counted eight rings on each rush stem.

"What is it?" she asked him.

"I haven't given it a name yet, I just call it a bark-rush thing. Do you like it?"

"Well, it's very neat and well made, but what's it for?"

She tipped it sideways and all the rings slid to one end.

Chip reached out and took it back. "It's for counting on," he said, his tail rising with pride. "Look."

His paws moved the rings back and forth along the rush stems so fast that Marguerite could hardly follow the action.

"There you are," he said, "that's a hundred." He shuffled the rings back and forth again. "And that's a thousand."

Chip passed the bark-rush thing to Marguerite. "You try," he invited.

By High-sun she was using it to count nearly as fast as he was, and each was trying out new ideas.

"Supposing we have a pair of squirrels," Chip said, "who have four dreylings each year for four years, we would have that many squirrels." He held the Bark-rush out to Marguerite.

"No we wouldn't," she told him, "each of those would be breeding, so we would have that many!" The rings flew backwards and forwards under her busy paws.

"Wow," said Chip. "That's a lot of squirrels!"

"Of course it's not true," Marguerite told him. "Foxes and other predators take many of us, that's a fact of squirrel life. Others will go off and live elsewhere and some may not have four dreylings every year. Even so, that's an oak-sized figure. Has any other squirrel seen this?"

"Not yet," he told her, "only you and I can count above eight, so it wouldn't mean much to them."

Marguerite went away, unable to get the picture of all those "calculated" squirrels out of her head. Chip was shuffling the rings again.

Marguerite wandered through the valley, past the broad-leaved palm trees, the last relics of some human's attempt to create a sub-tropical garden on the island, and up to the pines on the cliffs beyond. Here she lay out on a resin-scented branch enjoying the cool breeze coming in from the sea.

It was late afternoon and, just as she was thinking of going down to forage, her whiskers started twitching with the feeling that she now knew signalled that dolphins were near. She sat up and looked out over the harbour.

She could see three black heads and backs curving up out of the water and sliding down again, effortlessly keeping away from the few human boats that were sailing in on the tide. Then the thought-voices that she loved filled her head.

She heard Malin first. "Are you there, squirrel-friend?"

Marguerite thought back, "Yes, I am here," and the three heads immediately turned towards where she sat high above the beach.

Lundy's thought-waves reached her. "We are on our way up-channel to a school at the Goodwins and decided to swim into the harbour to see if all was well with you."

The dolphins and the squirrel exchanged pleasantries, then Lundy said, "We have been for a sea-change, down to the Island of Madeira. We could see blue trees on the land there, and I thought of you and how you would love to see them."

"Was it the leaves or flowers that made them blue?" Marguerite asked, intrigued.

"I think it was flowers, but they were too far away for us to be sure. The local dolphins call them Jacaranda trees."

Marguerite played with the name. She was so used now to communicating mentally that she could even sense the sounds of the thoughts. This blue tree had an exotic and exciting sound to it. Jacaranda, Jac-ar-an-da, Jacaranda.

"Did you meet many other dolphins?" she asked.

"Not as many as we have on earlier visits," Lundy replied sadly. "Humans are using a new kind of net which catches a lot of dolphins as well as fish. The nets are made of such thin lines that we can't detect them. It is easy to get entangled and then we drown."

Malin's voice flowed, swamping Lundy's. "Stop being a teredo. Our friend doesn't want to know all *our* problems."

Marguerite did not know how to respond, so asked, "What are you going to learn about at your school?"

"Actually we are to be the teachers on this session. You may recall that our patrol area is either side of the Rock of Portland. On the far side is a curved pebble beach that forms what we call the West Bay. Humans go there to catch fish with lines thrown out into the water. It was there that Malin discovered that when he goes near a line that is tautly stretched from a human's thin-stick out to the sea-bed, he can understand what *that* human is thinking."

"Is that a right thing to do?" asked Marguerite.

"We were not sure at first," Malin replied. "It did seem like an intrusion and while we are near their lines they don't catch any fish. But when we did listen we learned things which may help us understand them better; and *that* must be a good thing. I know that *you* often have difficulty in interpreting their actions."

"That's true."

> *People puzzle us*
> *With their strange actions. But then*
> *They're only human.*

"We often feel like that. So, on balance, we felt it was not wrong to listen."

"Have you learned anything important?" Marguerite asked.

"Much of interest, and we will tell you some of it when we return. Time is short for us now, and dolphins must never be late. I think we have told you our little reminder on this."

> *Punctuality*
> *Is vital. Others' time wasted,*
> *Is stolen by you*
> *And can never be returned.*
> *Lost minutes sink for ever.*

"Shall we swim in and tell you about the humans on our way back?"

"Yes please, if you would," said Marguerite; any new ideas thrilled her. She wished the dolphins farewell, then watched their black heads seem to get smaller as they swam for the harbour entrance and the open sea.

A sense of loneliness enveloped her as her sea-friends disappeared around North Haven Point.

Marguerite fed alone, then slept in one of the palm trees in the valley. The coarse fibres around the base of the leaves made a snug nest, but the unusual sound of the wind rustling the great flat leaves bothered her, and she slept badly. She dreamed of watching her friends, both squirrels and dolphins, drowning in nets. Waking from that dream, she drifted into another where the island was so densely populated with squirrels that several families had to share each tree.

She awoke shivering, even though the sun was above the horizon and the dawn air was pleasantly warm. She came down the trunk of the palm to forage, instinctively stopping well above the ground to look out for predators, before remembering that here on Ourland there were none. Realisation hit her like a peregrine falcon striking a pigeon.

As there were no predators on this island her second dream was likely to become a reality. Squirrels would multiply with no natural checks, and there was nowhere for the extra ones to go. Even if they could find a way to get back to the mainland, that was effectively grey squirrel country now, so was not an option. She went down to the Zwamp to find Chip.

He was rethreading a bark-ring to replace one that had broken, and, after the formal greeting, she asked him to re-do the calculations that they had done the previous day.

If each pair of squirrels . . .

They did many calcuations before resting at High-sun, and by then Chip was sharing Marguerite's concern. After her rest she went to find the Council Leader, Just Poplar.

He was at the Council Tree in Beech Valley with his life-mate, Rush the Kind. Rush had borne three dreylings that spring, two males and a female, half-brothers and a half-sister to Chip her first son. The youngsters were off with the others, probably playing the Wall-game.

After greeting and brushing whiskers with her friends, Marguerite tried to express her concern.

"Chip and I have been working out how many squirrels there will be if we all breed at the rate we are now. With no predators, the island will soon be overrun."

Just Poplar did not share her worries.

"Zumthing ztopz it happening," he told her. "In the old dayz uz Royalz wuz alwayz trying to have lotz of dreylingz but they moztly died and the zervantz never had too many. There alwayz zeemed to be about the right number of *them*. Don't yew worry now."

Rush offered Marguerite a piece of her favourite dried fungus and changed the subject.

"Lots of squirrels have stopped coming to Council Meetings," Rush said. "They all seem to be doing other things. We – Just Poplar and I – we don't know all the odd things that are going on."

"That'z true," Just Poplar added, "Uz'z zuppozed to be Leader and uz doezn't know if uz zhould encourage it or zupprezz it."

"What zort, sort of things?" Marguerite asked.

"Well, uz'z heard that Larch and hiz family are biting a tree into a zquirrel zhape over by Pottery Point, and that Chezdnud and Heather have got their clan growing Woodztockz. But Uz don't know how true it all iz."

"You sound like Chestnut the Doubter himself. He never believes anything unless he has seen it – at least twice."

31

They all smiled.

Marguerite bade them farewell and went through the trees to where Chestnut and Heather had their home near the ruined Man-dreys of Maryland. She found three generations of their family in a hazel copse digging up honeysuckle seedlings and replanting them at the foot of small hazel saplings.

"What are you doing?" she asked, though she could see for herself.

"Hello Marguerite," said Heather Treetops. "Chestnut doesn't believe that we and our family are safe here and so we are making sure we have plenty of Woodstocks to defend us all if Greys come here, or if a pine marten gets to the island again."

Marguerite looked at the young honeysuckles. Some were already reaching up and twisting round the hazel stems. She knew that in a year or two, a silent battle would commence between the encircling bine and the host sapling.

If the hazel grew fastest it would break the creeper, but the honeysuckle bine could strangle the sapling if it was the stronger. In either case the Life Force would be trapped while this was happening, forming the twisted whorl the squirrels knew as a Woodstock. It had been Marguerite who had learned how to release this trapped force with devastating effect, as many a Mainland Grey could tell.

She thanked Chestnut and Heather for showing her their plantation and headed for Pottery Point.

When the island's screen of protective trees loomed up ahead of her she remembered Wally's prophecy.

I honour birch-bark
The Island's screen. Flies stinging
The piece of the sun

Or should it be **A** piece? Either way it still seemed to be a nonsense.

Marguerite found Larch the Curious working with his sons, daughters and their youngsters biting at the wood of a broken tree and she stood and looked in amazement at what they had created.

The pine that had been broken off in the Great Storm had been chiselled by many teeth into the shape of a giant squirrel, staring out over the sea towards the Mainland. The face of the great animal scowled threateningly and it held a carved Woodstock diagonally across its chest.

Larch saw her, came over and brushed whiskers. She waited for him to explain.

"We got bored," he said, slightly embarrassed. "There is such a lot of food here, we don't have to spend much time foraging and we don't have to watch for predators, so we thought we'd make something. At least this should frighten any invaders away."

"Sun rule that no more come," Marguerite replied. "But this, this is . . ." she struggled for a word, "magnificent."

Larch stood proudly, his back to his creation.

"Where's Clover the Tagger?" Marguerite asked, looking round for Larch's life-mate.

"She's busy somewhere else. She doesn't really approve of all this," he added, waving a paw at the huge stump outlined against the setting sun. She thinks it's all a waste of time, but what is time anyway if you have plenty of it?

"A bite more off there," he called up to one of the busy youngsters, as Marguerite turned back along the shore towards the eastern end of the island.

Chapter 5

Marguerite spent several days in the South Shore area eating and sleeping alone. Twice she returned to the screen of trees above Pottery Point and from a distance watched the shaping of the giant squirrel progressing, but did not make contact with the chisellers. Her mind was busy with a web of ideas, trying to untangle thoughts that were hopelessly intertwined.

Early on the fifth morning, as the sun lifted over the eastern horizon and the tide surged in from Poole Bay, she knew, by the tingle in her whiskers, that the dolphins had come again. She went down to the low bank at the water's edge and projected her thoughts across the rippled surface of the harbour.

"I am here, my friends, I am here."

Three heads lifted above the wavelets in the quiet dawn-light and the two larger ones surged in towards her, while the smaller dolphin moved slowly up and down the waterway farther out.

Malin and Lundy rested in the shallows a few feet from Marguerite. She had never seen a dolphin at rest before and they looked huge, much bigger than a human.

"Hello, squirrel-friend," they said together, followed a moment later by a shyer greeting from Finisterre as he swam in.

"We promised to tell you what we learned from the fishing-men and we don't have to be back on patrol until tomorrow," Malin told her. "We decided to come early before any humans were about."

Lundy sent her thoughts up to Marguerite, "We told you that we often patrol just off the Chesil Bank and there are nearly always fishing-men on that beach trying to catch cod and conger eels. When we learned how to pick up their thoughts from the taut-lines, we were surprised to find that most are not even thinking about fish at all. Some come there just to get away from unhappy situations with their mates and others to relax and let their minds go blank. One was hiding his face behind a flimsy sheet of what they call paper all day, and his mind seemed full of nothing but enormous mammary glands. Then he stared out to sea, as if expecting a dugong to swim by."

Marguerite wondered briefly what a dugong was, but suppressed the thought. She was having a little difficulty in understanding, but wanted to know more.

"Why can't you just *know* what they are thinking, like you do with me?" she asked.

"You have an open mind," Lundy replied. "Humans try to keep their thoughts in a shell as though each was hiding some terrible secret. Only when they are alone on the beach do they relax and then their taut-lines convey their thoughts down into the sea like a trickle of water down a pipe."

"What else do they think about?" Marguerite asked.

Malin's thoughts washed in, "One was excited about things he was studying called 'computers'. You may know that humans in this part of the world do something called work which most don't like, for five days out of every seven and then they have two days for doing other things they do like, such as fishing. Then they do five more days of work."

"What is a computer?" Marguerite asked.

"It was hard to read that. I could only get a picture of a box, but it used numbers inside to find out all manner of things. That human was convinced that within a few years the computers would be doing much of the work the humans have to do now, and then they would share out what was left and each would be able to spend only four days doing work and have *three* days for fishing."

Overhead Marguerite heard the W-wow, W-wow sound of a swan's wing-beats and looked up as the great bird flew over. Finisterre's thoughts reached her. "I wish I could fly," he was thinking.

Malin said, "There will be humans about soon. We must go now."

"Are you going back out to sea?" Marguerite asked. "I've a friend I would like you to meet. Like me, he is interested in numbers."

"We plan to show Finisterre around Poole Harbour today – we could come back at dusk."

"I would like that," Marguerite said, and the dolphins wriggled backwards into deeper water and swam away up the harbour on the rising tide.

It was to be a long day for Marguerite. First she sought out Chip and tried to explain all that she had heard from the dolphins. She had told him before how she could communicate with them without actually speaking. Now she reminded him.

"I seem to be the only squirrel who can do it," she said.

"Not so," said Chip. "You remember when we were in that boat last year? I knew all that the dolphins were saying to you, but I couldn't hear what *you* were saying to them. Your mouth was shut all the time."

"You never told me this before," said Marguerite.

"I was always a bit scared of you then. You know – Tagger and all that." He smiled at her. "Now I know that you are just an ordinary squirrel like the rest of us . . . Ordinary, but special," he added.

Marguerite smiled back. "I often wish I could be *ordinary* – it's just that extra-ordinary things seem to keep happening to me."

Chip hung the latest version of the Bark-rush on a twig and sat back to listen to Marguerite's tale.

She told him, not only about the human's computer-box but about Chestnut and Heather's plantation of Woodstocks and the tree being made into a huge squirrel shape. "Sun knows what's going on in other parts of Ourland. We never get together as we used to, there are just too many of us. And since there's no danger now, it doesn't seem so important."

Chip looked grave. "I've done some more calculations," he told her. "In a few years time there will be more squirrels on this island than it can possibly support. I've tried to see what would happen if we increased the Sun's tithe and, even if we left half of the buried nuts to grow, there wouldn't be enough room on the island for all those trees. We're going to have to slow down our breeding rate, or find a way to get the extra squirrels to the Mainland."

"As far as we know, the Mainland is all Grey territory now. I don't know how they would react to us coming back," Marguerite said. "I often wonder how my brother Rowan and his party are doing. Only a squirrel as bold as he is would have dared to stay on and try to teach them *our* ideals. I worry about him a lot."

"He's got Meadowsweet, Spindle and Wood Anemone and all their youngsters with him; he's probably all right," Chip comforted her, but he knew from his own experiences that the Greys were unpredictable. Their morals and actions seemed to depend on who the Great Lord Silver was at their Woburn Base, and what that Great Lord believed was right, or expedient, at the time.

Marguerite's thoughts had moved on. "If we're going to get over to the South Shore in time to meet the dolphins, we'd better leave," she said.

Chip hid the Bark-rush and together they raced through the treetops in the gathering dusk, enjoying the activity and forgetting their worries in the pleasure of judging and executing graceful leaps between the trees.

The dolphins were waiting just off the beach.

"I'm sorry we're late," Marguerite panted, speaking the words out loud so that Chip could hear them as well as the dolphins. "I know that time is important to you. I remember you saying, *Lost minutes sink for ever.*"

"We have only just come ourselves," Lundy told her. "We waited until we could be sure that there were no humans about. They make such a fuss if they see us too close. Is that the friend you told us about?"

"Yes, like me he can understand your thoughts. I told him what you told me this morning. We both wish to hear more."

Marguerite and Chip settled in a tree near the shore. From there they could just see the shapes of the three dolphins in the water as the evening light faded and the tide started to ebb.

"We will have to move out farther as the tide falls," Lundy told them, "but darkness makes no difference to our conversation. Was there something you especially wanted us to tell you?"

"It's about that human's computer. Does it have rings of bark that move backwards and forwards on rush stems?"

"Not as far as we could tell. But the human only pictured the box that covered it. There might have been fish swimming backwards and forwards inside it for all we could tell."

Chip looked disappointed. "Do you think it will do what the humans want it to do?" he asked.

Malin appeared to be discussing something intimately with Lundy, shutting the squirrels out of their thoughts. Then he came back to them. "I once told you that dolphins can sometimes Look Forward but we don't often do it. I looked forward ⟨fish⟩/2 years to see if the human's predictions were correct."

Marguerite interrupted, "I'm sorry, but how long is ⟨fish⟩/2?"

"It is I who must apologize, I forgot that you count differently to us. ⟨fish⟩ is our symbol for what the humans would call sixty, so it would be one half of that. Thirty years to them."

Marguerite was about to interrupt again to point out that squirrels counted in eights, not tens as humans did, but suppressed the thought. She was far more interested in the dolphins' ability to Look Forward. Was this what Wally had been able to do?

"Was the man right about only four days of work and three days for fishing?"

"Sadly, no. He was right about computers taking over much of the work but the humans had *not* shared out what was left. Most were still working for five days out of seven and others were able to fish on all seven days. Our fishing-man was one of these, but he was not happy about it. Odd creatures, humans."

"I'm hungry." Finisterre's thoughts reached the squirrels. Marguerite smiled. All young males must be the same.

"Thank you, my friends," she said. "This has all been most interesting. I think your youngster wants to forage. Farewell and thank you again."

The dolphins turned in the darkness and swam for the open sea. Marguerite was glad that Chip was with her and the two of them climbed higher in the tree and settled down in a fork to discuss what they had learned, before drifting off to sleep, each enjoying the warm comfort of the other's body next to theirs.

Chapter 6

Marguerite had been glad of Chip's warmth. The night had been cold for sleeping alone in the open, and the sun was hidden behind low clouds when they woke and foraged together in a chill breeze from the sea.

They moved through the screen of trees, finding morsels of food here and there and, by the time they reached the old meadow they were comfortably full. Only occasionally did they sit up and look round, an unnecessary but still instinctive action, as they knew there were no predators to harm them. At the edge of the meadow they stopped.

"Look at all those rabbits," said Chip. "There must be a thousand."

The whole of the greensward was covered with hopping and nibbling animals. Some were sitting up, scratching at their long ears with their back feet. Others were brushing their whiskers back with their forepaws and a few were biting at the bark of young trees on the edge of the Screen.

Marguerite was angry. Grass was for rabbits – trees were the squirrel's charge. What the rabbits were doing would kill the saplings.

She ran at the ones nearest to her, chattering her anger

but, as soon as she turned away, they started nibbling the bark again.

"Come on," said Chip, "they're not taking any notice," and he led her away across the meadow, the lean rabbits opening a way to let them pass.

"No wonder they are eating bark; look – the grass has been eaten down to its roots."

All over the field there were scuff-marks and bare patches of earth, showing where even the roots themselves had been dug up.

On the far side of the meadow they rested in the bracken below a pine tree. Marguerite was calmer now and said the Understanding Kernel.

> *If you could know all*
> *Then you could understand all*
> *Then you'd forgive all.*

"Those poor creatures are starving!"

Later, with the help of Chip's Bark-rush, they calculated the breeding rate of rabbits on a predator-free island.

"If each pair of rabbits has a litter of eight, three times a year and each of these young ones has . . ."

The result was just what they had seen for themselves that morning in the meadow.

They tried the squirrel calculation again.

"If each pair of squirrels has . . ."

The result at six generations was not as bad as at six generations of rabbits, but it was clearly far more than the island could ever support. Marguerite imagined squirrels as lean and as hungry as the rabbits, and looked at Chip in horror. "We must do something," she said.

Something was already being done as far as the rabbits were concerned. A newly-dead corpse of a mainland rabbit had been surreptitiously laid in an island rabbit-hole by a human, and the fleas were leaving the cooling body to seek a living host. The fleas were themselves hosts to a virus, known to humans as myxomatosis.

A few days later Marguerite was telling Ex-Kingz-Mate Thizle of her concern about the likelihood of there soon being too many squirrels on the island.

"Why didn't the squirrels overpopulate the island before we came?" she asked the dignified old Ex-Royal.

"The King dizcouraged it."

"Discouraged what?" Marguerite asked, "Mating?"

"Oh no. Him encouraged that zure-enuff; said it was good for zquirrelz. Him wuz fond of that himzelf. No, what him dizcouraged wux zervantz having too many dreylingz."

"But if they mated, surely there were dreylings later?"

"Zumhow not, uz forgetz why now." Thizle shifted uncomfortably.

Marguerite felt that the old squirrel was holding something back and said, "I'm afraid that if there are too many squirrels a plague will come, like it has with the rabbits. Have you seen them?"

"Yez, poor beasties, hopping round blind until they are Zun-gone. A relief for them then. No zquirrel huz caught it, huz they?"

"Nothing has been reported. But all squirrels have been warned to keep away from the rabbits, even if they seem well. The humans are collecting all the bodies they can find and burying them."

Thizle changed the subject. Marguerite had noticed on previous visits how the old squirrel could not concentrate on one thing for very long.

"Yew rememberz that Kernel yew azked uz about? Old Wally's prophezy."

Marguerite nodded. A pigeon flew into their tree, perched unsteadily on a brach too thin for it, was about to hop to another, then, seeing the squirrels so close, flew off again with a loud clapping of its wings.

Old Thizle's thoughts seemed to have flown away with it.

"What wuz uz talking about? Oh yez, Wally'z Kernel. Well, uz'z been thinking about that. Maybe the I'land'z Zcreen should be the I'land'z Queen."

"What's a Queen?" Marguerite asked.

"Her'z a vemale King. If the eldezd Royal youngzter is a vemale, her becomz Queen when the King is Zun-gone."

Marguerite recited the Kernel using the new words.

I honour birch-bark
The Island's Queen. Flies stinging
The piece of the sun.

"Like that, it sounds as though the Queen was called Birch-bark. Is that possible?"

"No, my dear," the old squirrel said affectionately. "Vemales uz alwayz named after flowerz and the malez after treez like yew lot duz. Birch-bark izn't a flower."

Her eyelids were drooping and she was glancing towards the entrance of her drey. Marguerite tried to turn the conversation back to the subject that concerned her but Thizle was asleep. She left quietly.

Near the Zwamp Chip was working on the Bark-rush.

"What are you calculating this time?" she asked.

"Bumblebees," he said.

"Bumblebees?"

"Yes." He pointed at what looked like a mouse's hole in the bank beside him. A female bumblebee, with brown and buff bands across its body, buzzed past their heads and landed heavily at the edge of the hole, pads of pollen bright gold on her legs.

The bee paused for a moment, then crawled into the hole.

"I've done some calculations," he said. "I've taken the size of its wings and the probable weight of its body and the fastest rate at which it can possibly beat its wings. See."

Chip slid the bark-rings back and forth along the rush stems, Marguerite straining to keep up with the calculations.

"Can it beat them that fast?" she asked.

"Just possible, I should think," said Chip. "Certainly no faster. But look what the result is!"

"What?" asked Marguerite.

"It can't fly," said Chip. "It's quite impossible."

"But we've just seen it fly," said Marguerite.

"I know, but I've done the calculations many times and I always get the same answer – it can't fly."

"I'll believe you," said Marguerite, "but don't tell the

46

Bumblebee. While it doesn't know it can't, it'll keep on flying."

> *If you think you can*
> *Or if you think you cannot*
> *Either way it's true.*

Chapter 7

It was well into summer and the days were hot and lazy. In the Tanglewood the elderly grey squirrels who still called themselves the Three Lords were lying out on the highest branches hoping for a caressing breeze.

"You two keep saying that you will come with me to see what the world is doing since the plague, but you never do," Lord Malachite grumbled.

"Go on your own then," said Lord Silica, "I'm comfortable here."

"What about you?" Malachite asked Lord Obsidian.

"Go to – sleep," was the only reply he received.

Malachite stretched and shut his eyes. Visions of the ambition of his youth filled his mind. He was the Great Lord Silver, seated outside the Oval Drey at Woburn Headquarters surrounded by a retinue of adoring acolytes and females ready to serve him and fulfil his every wish. Tomorrow, *he* was going to leave the Tanglewood whether or not the others came with him.

The cooing of the pigeons announced the dawn. Lord Malachite waited impatiently until his compatriots came out of their dreys to forage.

"We are leaving today," Malachite announced, hoping that the sound of authority in his voice would suppress any thought of resistance, and was relieved and a little surprised when Silica and Obsidian appeared to conform though they insisted on eating first.

After some discussion and bickering about the exact direction, they headed almost due east, backtracking on the route they had used years ago, after setting up the Power Square.

Malachite was sure that they had only taken one day when they had fled from the Clay-Pan to the Tanglewood but, as dusk fell, they were still some way from their objective, and had to stop and spend a night in a hedgerow tree before moving on soon after daybreak.

They crossed the roadway near to the Blue Pool and wriggled through the hedge into the Dogleg Field. There was no sign of humans, though two horses were grazing there, one white and black in large irregular patches, the other the colour of a ripe chestnut in autumn. As the squirrels slipped through the grass, the horses approached, head down, sniffing and snorting at the little animals they usually only saw in the trees on the other side of the field.

The Three Lords hurried on, to stop, breathless, when they reached the safety of that wood.

"Stupid great creatures," said Lord Silica when they had recovered somewhat. "Come on. The Clay-Pan is this way."

Standing on the edge of the shallow depression where they had once directed the laying out of the stones, they could see the shattered trunk and the decaying branches of the fir which had destroyed the alignment of the stones and hence the power of the great Square.

Lizards basked on the gleaming white cakes of clay. Malachite stalked one which was sleeping in the sunshine. He slashed out at it, pinning its tail to the ground. The lizard ran off, leaving the end of its tail writhing under the squirrel's paw. Malachite flicked it away.

"All that work for nothing," said Obsidian, forgetting that it was ordinary Greys who had actually built the Square, while the Three Lords themselves had stood on the bank supervising.

"No squirrels round here now," Silica observed, sniffing the air.

"Let's try the Blue Pool itself."

They passed the Little Pool, over which gaudy dragon-flies hawked for gnats and other insects, then cautiously approached the Blue Pool. Soon they could look down onto the water, sparkling and sapphire-coloured under the late morning sun.

Human visitors were walking on the sandy paths below them, and although there was the scent of grey squirrels in the trees, surprisingly, there was also the scent of Reds as well.

"Can you smell natives – Reds?" Silica asked.

"I think I can, but they shouldn't be here, especially if Greys are in occupation," Malachite replied.

The three circled the Pool, passing behind the Man-dreys, and eventually saw a group of squirrels, including both Reds and Greys, in a tree on the edge of the North-east Wood. They watched for a while, then moved forward.

Rowan the Bold looked to where Hickory was pointing.

"Welcome," he called. "Come and join us."

The elderly greys came forward and he greeted them formally. "I am Rowan the Bold." He turned to a Red female beside him. "This is my life-mate Meadowsweet Rowan's Love, and these," he indicated two other Red assistants, "are Wood Anemone the Able and Spindle the Helpful. This is Hickory, one of your own kind, and all of these – these are Greys learning our ways, here at Blue Pool Base, as directed by your Great Lord Silver."

The Three Lords glanced at one another, then Malachite stepped forward.

"I am Lord Malachite, this is Lord Silica and this is Lord Obsidian. We greet you in the name of the Great Lord Silver." Malachite held his right paw diagonally across his chest and Silica and Obsidian did the same.

Rowan could feel Meadowsweet trembling on the branch beside him. "Are you the Three Lords who ordered my father's group to head for the sea when you found us on that barrow?" she asked, trying to keep her voice steady.

"It could have been, we met a lot of your kind then. Did your father have no tail?"

"Yes," Meadowsweet replied. "One of your kind broke it."

Silica stepped forward. "If we told you to go to the sea, what are you doing here?" he asked fiercely.

Meadowsweet did not answer, but moved behind Rowan, who asked, "If you are those same Three Lords, how did you escape the Power Square? Marble told us that he saw you overcome by the power-waves at the Clay-Pan."

"Is Marble Threepaws here?" Silica asked, looking round. "I thought the Grey Death would have got him."

"He died helping us destroy your Power Square," Rowan replied. "How did you escape?"

"We were caught by the waves and thrown down the bank," Obsidian told him, "but we crawled into a rabbit hole and found a way out through a bolt-hole to the Heath. We've been resting since then. What is going on here?"

Hickory came forward and explained.

"Sirs, the new Great Lord Silver directed all of our kind to learn the ways of the native Reds and live like they do, but when we got to this place there was a misunderstanding, and we fought with Rowan and his companions. They used a weapon called a Woodstock and beat us. Since then we have been learning native ways and teaching these to all the colonising Greys passing through."

"You let natives teach you!" exploded Malachite. "Natives!"

Rowan looked offended, then, realising that these three had been in isolation and were out of touch, he relaxed. They did not look fit enough to be a danger.

The Greys whose class was being disrupted, giggled and nudged one another as they saw this overweight and aged grey squirrel making a fool of himself. All that the Reds had taught them so far was very sensible and in tune with how things were, here in New America. The Kernels of Truth they had learned held subtle messages to guide behaviour, and Rowan and his companions were able and patient teachers. No doubt this fat stranger and his paunchy friends would soon be sent away.

"Would the three of you like to join our class?" Rowan

asked. "We are discussing Leadership. This morning we learned the Kernel:

> *In any crisis*
> *A Leader's first duty, is –*
> *To keep hope alive.*

"Did you know that one?" he asked Silica.

"Of course I did, we all do," Silica mumbled. "Get on with it."

Meadowsweet moved forward. "Today I am going to tell you a story that makes an important point about leadership. It is one my great grandfather used to tell in the old days at Wolvesbarrow before. . ." she paused, "before things changed."

The three settled on the branch, the sun hot on their backs.

Chapter 8

Meadowsweet started her story. The Three Lords appeared to be dozing and she thought that Silica was snoring, but it might just be that he was having difficulty breathing. She had seen this problem with elderly squirrels before.

"Once upon a time," she started, using the time-honoured wording, "at a place called Gaudier, where the leaves were a brighter colour than anywhere else in the world, the old leader was Sun-gone and no other squirrel had been selected to succeed him. In Gaudier they had a Kernel that said:

> Whichever squirrel
> Solves the challenge of the Knot,
> Will be the leader.

"The Knot had been made many years before by their Bard and Sage, who was also Sun-gone. Before he died he had tied stringy cherry bark into a great tangled knot, and left it out to weather.

"By the time it came to choose a leader no squirrel could undo that knot no matter how hard they tried.

"Then a bright young squirrel called Zander came along and asked what they were doing. No one has ever explained to me why a squirrel was named after a fish rather than a tree, but that's not the point.

"Young Zander took one look at the Knot and *bit* it through and so they made him their leader. He was very successful, because it is important in a leader to see different ways of solving challenges and not just to do what everyone else is doing. Zander's daring exploits earned him a new tag and ever since he has been remembered as Zander the Great.

"Are there any questions on that story?" Meadowsweet asked, looking expectantly at the assembled Greys.

"Surely what he did was against the rules?" a Grey asked.

"Not really," Meadowsweet replied. "The Kernel just said *Solve the challenge of the Knot*, it didn't say *Untie the Knot*. The others just assumed that is what they had to do and, as we learned yesterday, it is dangerous to 'assume'. Who can remember that Kernel?"

Several Greys raised their paws and Meadowsweet chose one near the back to answer.

> *Squirrels who don't check,*
> *May "assume" a fox's mouth*
> *To be a safe den.*

"Correct," said Meadowsweet and the Grey looked pleased with himself.

55

"Rubbish," Silica mumbled, only half awake. "Rules are meant to be broken – do whatever you can get away with. Might is right – so fight."

Meadowsweet glanced at Rowan.

"I think we have learned enough for today. We'll meet here again tomorrow after dawn-foraging. You are welcome to join us if you wish," he said to the Three Lords.

"We'll see, we'll see," Malachite replied. "Where do we sleep if we should decide to stay?"

"There are dreytels in the wood over there," she said, the ugly word harsh on her tongue. Greys seemed to prefer these characterless one-squirrel structures to the traditional, comfortable, communal dreys whilst they were studying here, or when they stopped off in passing.

The Reds, as they always had, still used a drey for each of their families on Steepbank near the Blue Pool.

The next morning, to Meadowsweet's surprise, the Three Lords did come back to the class, taking their places quietly among the other Greys.

She asked for a volunteer to retell the story of Zander the Great and the Gaudian knot and she was flattered when Lord Malachite recited almost word for word what she had said the day before.

She thanked him, and Rowan was about to move on to the Action Kernel when there was a disturbance in the treetops and Sitka, Hickory's assistant, leapt into their tree.

"There's a *new* Great Lord Silver at Woburn," he announced breathlessly. "A batch of colonists have just arrived and told me all about it. A Grey from a place called Seven Oaks arrived at the Oval Drey at dawn with a band of supporters, and challenged the Great Lord Silver to fight for his position. The challenger didn't even wait for a reply; just pitched straight in and had Redwood's tail off before he was fully awake, but they say he's quite an old squirrel himself and may not last for long."

There was a murmur of excitement from the class. Each knew that a change of occupant at the Oval Drey meant a change of policy. At least Redwood's had been benign. What changes would this new leader bring?

"What's the name of the new Great Lord?" Hickory asked Sitka.

"Monterey," said Sitka. "By all accounts his views are very different to Redwood's. Some are saying that he doesn't believe in the *Learn from the Natives* policy. It might be back to the *Take and Hold* philosophy again."

Rowan moved closer to Meadowsweet and put a paw on her shoulder.

"The class is dismissed for the day," he announced and, looking frequently over his shoulder, he led Meadowsweet away to find their daughter, Bluebell, and the ex-zervantz and their two daughters, Rosebay and Willowherb. They found them replacing the moss used for the linings of their dreys in the tree they all shared on Steepbank, next to the Blue Pool.

"We have a new challenge," Rowan said and went on to tell what he had just heard, and explain its significance.

"I think we would be wise to slip away and try and get back to Ourland somehow. Before we're missed. You can't trust these Greys when there's instability at their Headquarters."

"That doesn't sound like my Rowan the Bold," said

Meadowsweet. "I've never known you to 'slip away', as you put it. Are we just going to abandon all the good work we've put in here. If we've done a worthwhile job the Greys won't harm us; we've taught them most of the Kernels."

Rowan looked ashamed. "Sorry," he said, "I panicked – not like me – sorry."

"What *should* we do then?" asked Spindle, hoping for firm leadership from his hero, Rowan.

"I'll go and talk to these new colonists – find out all I can."

"I'll come with you," said Spindle.

Rowan turned to Meadowsweet. "Go down to the Little Pool, all of you. Stay out of sight. We'll be back by High-sun."

High-sun passed and Rowan and Spindle did not return. The females waited through the long afternoon, their concern growing as the shadows of the trees grew longer.

Chapter 9

"I think we should pray," said Meadowsweet as the sun dipped below the horizon and there was still no sign of Rowan and Spindle.

The five squirrels bowed their heads and followed Meadowsweet as she said:

> *Oh great loving Sun*
> *We are in need of guidance*
> *Please enlighten us.*

They sat as though expecting something to happen immediately.

"We will have to wait until morning," Meadowsweet said brightly. "We musn't worry. Several of the Greys are friends and Rowan is good at overcoming challenges."

She had herself taught Leadership Kernels to the Greys, but had never imagined herself in this situation.

> *When the cones are down*
> *Even if you doubt yourself*
> *Hide all your concerns.*

The squirrels crouched together on a branch. It was a warm and slightly moist night, typical of early August. Each dozed a little but they were uneasy, listening hopefully for the sound of Rowan and Spindle's return, but also fearing the approach of danger in the darkness.

"What's that?" whispered Bluebell.

"I didn't hear anything," Meadowsweet replied.

"No. Over there – what is it?"

Meadowsweet sensed the direction her daughter was facing and peered into the darkness. On the far side of the Little Pool something was glowing greeny-white in the darkness.

All of them were alert and apprehensive now, and each could see the mysterious light. They watched it, all the while whispering to each other, but it did not move nor seem to threaten them in any way. As long as it stayed on the ground on the far side of the pool they knew it was safest to stay where they were until daybreak.

Dawn came with a light mist obscuring the sun and Meadowsweet was thinking of a break-fast meal when she heard a rustling of pine needles in the next tree.

"Rowan?" she called tentatively.

"No, it's me – Hickory." A grey face with rounded ears peered out of the foliage.

"Where are Rowan and Spindle?" Meadowsweet asked, the other females all sitting up in a row on the branch beside her.

Hickory leapt across to their tree and looked behind him before speaking.

"They're being held while it is decided what to do with them. I don't think they're in danger at present. They are under guard in the Warren Ash."

Meadowsweet knew the Warren Ash tree. It was the over-mature ash tree in the North-east Wood, so named because it grew out of a sandy bank riddled with rabbit-holes, which, since the Rabbit Plague, were now deserted and empty. There was a squirrel-sized hole in the trunk of the ash tree which the Reds had used as a weather-proof storage chamber in the past and as a refuge in the Great Storm of that spring.

Greys had enlarged the hole to allow their bigger bodies to squeeze through when they had pillaged all the Reds' reserves in the days of Crag the Temple Master. The large cavity inside was floored with powdered punkwood which filled the trunk to a couple of tail-lengths below the entrance.

"I must go now, or I'll be missed," Hickory said. "If I learn anything more I'll try to get away and tell you. Trust in the Sun."

So Hickory has become a Sun-squrriel like us, Meadowsweet thought. I can believe what he says.

"Thank you," she called after him. "The Sun be with you." Then turning to her companions she said, "Who's coming with us to see what was making the light we saw in the night?"

They all circled the Little Pool, keeping together in the treetops until they were above the place where they agreed they had seen the mysterious glow.

"There's nothing here but a rotten log."

Wood Anemone had climbed down to investigate. She poked at the soft fibres, damp from the mist. They smelt mouldy and particles came away on her paw. She rubbed it

61

against her belly fur and then tried to brush off the crumbs of wood that stuck there.

"Come on up," Meadowsweet called to her, "we'll go and see if we can contact Rowan and Spindle. Move quietly now."

"Kill them both," said Lord Malachite. "Natives are just a nuisance. The only good native is a dead one!"

"There can't be many Reds left now," said Lord Silica. "It'd be a pity to kill them all. Perhaps we could make a reserve for them to live in. Our youngsters could go and look at them and know what New America was like before we came."

"They'd only breed and then we'd have the same problem again."

"We don't know yet what the new Great Lord Silver's attitude to natives is," Lord Obsidian said. "I think we should keep them under guard until we know that. We'd better capture the females." He turned to Sitka. "How many of those are there?"

Sitka hesitated for a moment, then replied, "Five. There's Rowan's mate, Meadowsweet, and their daughter, Bluebell; and Spindle's mate, Wood Anemone, and their two daughters, Rosebay and Willowherb. Those two are identical – I can never tell which is which."

"All natives look the same to me," said Malachite. "Useless creatures the lot of them."

"That's not true," said Hickory, whose absence and return had been unobserved. "You can't make broad-leaved statements like that. The ones I know are honourable and decent. They should be judged by their standards, not ours."

"So you're a native-lover are you?" sneered Malachite.

"I'm just trying to be fair, but I agree with Lord Obsidian. We should keep the red males secure while we learn what Woburn's views are. The females are not likely to go far away while we are holding their males."

Malachite was thinking of how exciting it would be when he was the Great Lord Silver, with the whole of Grey-Squirreldom in New America waiting on his pleasure and responding to his every whim. Young Grey males were taught that the position was attainable by any one of them.

"Anyone know where the females are?" Lord Obsidian asked.

The Greys shook their heads, except Hickory who was scratching and biting at some irritation on his back, his face buried in his fur.

The females, moving cautiously in a single file led by Meadowsweet, were nearing the Warren Ash. They made a pretty sight as they moved through the treetops. A weak sun was just breaking through the mist, lighting up their glossy fur. Each squirrel was well groomed and tidy, though none were as fanatical as Rowan's mother, Fern the Fussy, had been. Their tails were clear of tangles and their claws neat and clean. There was just a suspicion of the ear tufts that made the Reds so distinctive in winter.

"If you see any Greys – freeze," Meadowsweet whispered.

When they were in view of the Warren Ash they stopped and watched. Two Greys who they did not recognise were on guard, one on either side of the hole which showed up clearly where squirrel's teeth had over many years, worked to keep the bark from growing and closing it.

Meadowsweet quoted the Reconnaissance Kernel:

> *In a strange country,*
> *Be careful. Time spent looking*
> *Is seldom wasted.*

They crouched and observed, unnoticed by the guards.

Soon two other Greys came and relieved these. Both of the new guards stayed near the entrance hole.

"Does anyone know if there are any other openings in the tree?" Meadowsweet asked hopefully.

"There izn't any otherz," Wood Anemone whispered back. "Uz knowz that tree well. Uz uzed to keep uz nutz there wuntz."

Meadowsweet was looking at the many big holes in the ground around the base of the tree, remembering when she and her parents had lived in rabbit holes three summers before. "Follow me," she said, "quietly."

They approached the warren from the side away from the guards and slipped unseen into the first entrance they came to. It seemed very dark inside, then as their eyes became accustomed to the dim light they were able to look around. Meadowsweet was especially interested in the roots which showed through the roofs of the tunnels.

"Most hollow trees are hollow right to the ground," she told her companions. "If this one is, then we may be able to dig up through the soil from below."

"Thiz wun izn't," said Wood Anemone. "It'z vull of punkwood."

"Yes, but that's soft, we can dig through that easily."

64

Then looking at Wood Anemone, she said, "What's that on your belly?"

They all looked. Her belly fur and right paw were glowing in the darkness.

"It muzd be zum of that rotten wood uz all zaw lazd night. Uz muzd have got zum on uz fur." She brushed it violently.

"Wait," Meadowsweet told her. "The Sun has heard our prayer. We asked to be enlightened, it looks as if you have been. Come with me, all of you."

An hour later they were back, travelling on the ground, avoiding the human visitors near the pool and each bringing as much of the damp rotten wood as they could carry. Inside the warren they made a heap which glowed brightly, giving off enough light to show their faces clearly.

"We may take some time to complete the rescue," Meadowsweet said. "Wood Anemone, will you take Rosebay and Willowherb and collect all the food you can carry and bring it in here. Watch out for Greys. Bluebell and I will try and see if we can follow the roots back to the tree.

Each squirrel is free
To choose its own root through Life
Guided by Kernels.

It gives a whole new meaning to that."

Meadowsweet heard the others chuckling and saw Rosebay nudge Willowherb. Two jokes in as many hours;

65

she had never been known to tell even one. The twins followed their mother out into the open, still smiling.

Bluebell took a large piece of rotten wood and held the glowing mass up near the tunnel roof. She could clearly see the roots and tried to judge which was the thicker end. Mother and daughter followed the twisting tunnels, stopping frequently to study the root shapes.

"Meadowsweet-Ma," Bluebell said suddenly, "how will we find our way back?"

Meadowsweet stepped to one side and Bluebell could see her smiling over the bundle of rotten wood she was holding. Back down the passage that they had just followed, a line of glowing dots shone in the darkness. Meadowsweet broke off another piece and dropped it on the floor of the tunnel.

"I think the roots are getting smaller again," Bluebell said. "We must have passed under the tree."

They circled round in various tunnels until they were sure that they were at the most likely place. Meadowsweet reached up and scratched at the roof. A shower of dry soil and powdered wood enveloped her.

"This is it," she said. "We'll leave a marker here and get the others."

They laid out the shape of one of Marguerite's Xs on the ground with the last of the wood they had carried with them, and followed the glowing fragments back to the entrance. The other three had already returned with food which they shared out and ate. Each squirrel then took a piece of shining wood and followed the markers to where the X indicated the centre of the tree trunk above them. Meadowsweet reached up and scrabbled some of the punkwood down into the tunnel. The fine dry dust enveloped them and they coughed as it filled their throats and lungs. It was dry and bitter on their tongues.

Taking it in turns, they pulled more and more of the powdery punkwood down into the tunnel, the others pushing and carrying it away into side passages.

"If the rabbits ever come back, they won't be very pleased," Bluebell said.

"Never mind the rabbits, it's Rowan and Spindle who are important today – keep digging," Meadowsweet told her.

The squirrels were covered in fine dust and particles of the incandescent wood. They all glowed as they dug upwards, the glowing particles giving off just enough light to see by.

Meadowsweet looked up to where she imagined the Sun to be and breathed a heartfelt "Thank you", totally unaware that the sun was on the other side of the world and it was now completely dark outside.

Above them Rowan shook Spindle awake.

"I'm going to see if the guards are still there," he whispered.

"Yes, be careful," Spindle responded, needlessly.

Rowan had looked out once during the day, only to have his face savagely slashed by a grey paw.

He climbed up from the soft punkwood floor and reached a tentative paw out of the hole. It touched fur, and teeth nipped it hard. Rowan withdrew his paw, trying not to cry out. He dropped back down to the bottom of the hollow and licked away the blood. It was salty on his tongue and he felt thirsty.

Spindle was scratching in the darkness.

"Do yew think uz could tunnel out? Uz don't remember a hole lower down in thiz tree but anything iz better than zitting here doing nothing."

"There isn't another hole. I know this tree well," Rowan replied, then regretted saying it. Here was an ex-zervant showing initiative and he, Rowan the so-called Bold, was pouring cold water on the idea.

"You're right," he said, "anything's better than just sitting here. There may be a hole we don't know about." He started to dig.

At first it was easy. Under the top layer of finely powdered wood was a layer of empty hazel-nut shells and a few dry leaves which crackled as they moved them.

"Quiet," hissed Rowan. "We don't want to alert the guards."

As the hole they were making got deeper, their challenge was how to dispose of the debris. They piled it around the sides of the chamber but soon the debris started to trickle down on them and they had to lift it out again. Eventually a pile of fine powder poured down onto Spindle and buried him. He wriggled up, coughing and spluttering. Then all the stacked punkwood slid down into the hole and filled it. Rowan and Spindle climbed up to the inside of the entrance hole and hung there precariously hoping to find clearer air.

"What are you two doing?" a gruff voice called from outside.

Below them, the females were making better progress, gravity being on their side. There were frequent cascades of powdered wood, mixed with the scales and dried remains of insects and the occasional leaf or nut-shell. The glow from the particles of rotten wood on their fur allowed them to see what they were doing and avoid the worst of the dust-falls. Even so they were tiring and the rate at which they were moving the rubbish away was slowing noticeably.

Then with a whoosh of sound, a huge mass of punk-wood fell, covering those working below, and pitching a bewildered Rowan and Spindle down onto the wriggling bodies of the five females who were struggling to free themselves.

A rush of cool air passed them, drawn up the tree as if it were a chimney. A stream of fine powder poured out of the hole past the guards.

"What's going on in there?" a voice from outside called huskily and the squirrels below tried not to cough.

"Which way is out?" Rowan asked the glowing figure of his life-mate as they embraced.

Hearing no sound from within the tree for at least a minute, one of the guards cautiously pushed his head into the hole, even darker inside than the night around him. He withdrew it rapidly, his eyes full of dust. The other guard, who had gone round the tree to see if he could find out what had made that odd whooshing noise, rubbed his eyes as he saw what appeared to be a line of glowing squirrel-shapes materialise from nowhere in the darkness below him, then scurry towards the pine trees. He watched them fade away between the trunks before returning to his companion.

"Did you see anything?" he was asked.

"No," he replied, his voice high and a little shaky. "Nothing at all."

An owl hooted derisively and the squirrel shivered.

Chapter 10

"Do any of you have anything to say before we consider a tag change?"

Clover the Tagger looked at the three youngsters on the branch before her, then at the assembled squirrels of the Council. There were many gaps. Apologies had been sent by squirrels busy on various projects. Larch had sent a message saying he was at a critical stage on his carving. The ex-princesses, Voxglove and Cowzlip the Carers, had responded by saying that they were building a special drey where sick squirrels could be treated and that ex-prince Fir was helping them that day by testing different plants for healing properties.

Heather Treetops had just sent word to say that she and Chestnut were "unavailable", but there was a sprinkling of ex-zervantz, though again no Caterpillar. Marguerite was there with Chip, as were Just Poplar and Alder, but very few of that year's new generation were present, although they were entitled and even encouraged to attend.

The three youngsters had been found, ruddled and helpless, at the leaf pile and when sober, had been summoned to appear before the Council.

One of the offenders, Sycamore, sat up, tail high.

"Yes," he said. "There's nothing for us to do on this Sun-damned island. We just get bored. It was all right for you lot, you could go on climbabout when you lived on the Mainland. We can't. And it must have been exciting when that pine marten was here. Nothing like that happens here now. It's all so dull. That's all."

Clover looked at Marguerite then back at the youngsters.

"Does anyone else have anything to say?"

The other young squirrels shook their heads, so she sent the three out of ear-twitch and looked around at those who had attended, most clearly taken aback by the lack of respect shown.

"Do we have any choice but to tag them 'Ruddled'?" she asked.

"Perhaps Sycamore should be 'the Ruddled and Disrespectful'," Marguerite suggested.

"Where have you been?" Clover replied sharply. "Most of them are like that, I really don't know what to do. It'll just have to be 'the Ruddled' and we must hope they will grow out of it."

The three were called back and told that each would have to bear the low-tag "the Ruddled". They turned to leave, led by Sycamore, their tails high.

"Wait," said Clover the Tagger. "You have been downtagged, lower your tails. You are in disgrace."

"What about him then?" asked Sycamore, pointing to Chip. "He's supposed to be Chip the Ruddled, but he goes around with Miss Hoity-Toity, his tail as high as ever."

Without waiting for an answer, Sycamore dropped to the ground and sauntered off.

Marguerite looked around to see who Miss Hoity-Toity was, then realised with horror that Sycamore had been referring to her. Was that what they called her behind her back? She looked at Just Poplar; he was engrossed in conversation with Alder, and Clover was on her way to join them. Chip had slipped away unnoticed. Feeling angry and left out, she went quietly down the tree trunk alone.

Another group of dreylings were playing at The Wall as she passed, and she realised with a shock that Sycamore the Ruddled had been among those she had watched here, earlier in the year. These playing the game now were youngsters from Second Litters. Were these dear little ones, going to grow up loutish, like the three at the Council Meeting? Would *they* think of her as Miss Hoity-Toity? She heard the chant coming from behind her.

> *I honour birch-bark*
> *The island screen. Flies stinging . . .*

The Island's Queen . . . She corrected mentally then turned to seek the Ex-Kingz-Mate. Marguerite was sure that the old Royal knew something that she might be persuaded to tell.

Ex-Kingz-Mate Thizle was not on her branch in the sunshine when she arrived at her drey so Marguerite said the Calling Kernel:

> *Hello and greetings*
> *I visit you and bring peace.*
> *Emerge or I leave.*

73

She waited, ready to go if there was no response.

"Marguerite," called a feeble voice from within the drey. "Come yew in, please. Uz'z glad to zee yew."

Marguerite wriggled in through the entrance and found the old squirrel inside, very feeble and weak.

"Thank the Zun yew came," Thizle said, struggling to pronounce the words. "Uz'll be Zun-gone zoon and ther'z zumthing uz muzd tell yew."

Marguerite propped her up and tried to make her comfortable. "Yes," she said, "I'm listening. What is it?"

"Woodlowz knows . . ." The old squirrel stopped and Marguerite repeated her words.

"Woodlouse knows . . ."

"How the muzhroomz of the moon . . ."

Marguerite repeated this, "How the mushrooms of the moon . . ."

There was a long pause, Thizle breathing with difficulty.

Marguerite waited.

"Controlz the breeding." The words were very faint and indistinct.

"Controls the bleeding?" Marguerite queried.

"No, no! Controlz . . ."

Thizle's head fell back against Marguerite's shoulder and the old Ex-Kingz-Mate drew a last rattling breath and slumped down on the mossy lining of her drey.

Marguerite put a paw on Thizle's thin chest. It was still.

She laid the body out straight and went to tell the others and to get help to carry the body down to the ground for burial. The loss of her friend and confidante left her feeling as though a piece had been painfully bitten out of her own chest.

"Woodlouse knows how the mushrooms of the moon controls the bleeding." Marguerite repeated the message again and again as she went. Was that what Thizle had said? It was almost as confusing as Wally's prophecy about honouring birch-bark.

Woodlouse was the original name the Royals had given to her friend Wood Anemone, one of their zervants who was now on the Mainland with Rowan. What did *she* know about the Moon Mushrooms, whatever these were? And how did they control bleeding? Why had old Thizle suddenly thought it important to tell her about them as she was dying?

Marguerite had reached the Council Tree.

"Clover. Old Thizle is Sun-gone. I've just come from her drey."

Thizle was buried at the foot of her drey-tree and most of the island squirrels were present. One of the ex-zervants had brought along a small feather from a peacock's tail, with a gleaming eye in the fan, similar to the feather once carried so proudly by Thizle in the days when she was Kingz-Mate.

Thizle's son, Just Poplar, took the feather and laid it alongside the body of his mother before saying the Farewell Kernel:

> *Sun, take this squirrel*
> *Into the peace of your earth*
> *To nourish a tree.*

Chapter 11

Hickory was waiting at the Little Pool when the Reds arrived back, tired and dirty, in the early dawn.

He listened to the story of the escape and looked at Meadowsweet with a new respect. To think what that old fool Malachite had said about natives!

"What do you plan to do now?" he asked Rowan.

"We'll need to get cleaned up first," he said, seeing his life-mate looking ruefully at her claws, torn and broken from the night's digging, "then decide on action."

> *Indecision kills.*
> *Act positively and lead.*
> *Action is the Key.*

"We can't stay here," Rowan went on, "but it'll be the third time in four years that you Greys have driven me out. It's getting to be routine. Do any of the others know you're here?"

"No, I thought of telling Sitka but I'm not sure if I can trust him. I think he's got ambitions to be the Great Lord

Silver and he might believe it would go against him if he was known to have assisted natives."

"Don't you have that ambition?" asked Rowan.

"Not now. I used to once, but I've learned a lot from your teachings and there are more important things to me now." He glanced across at Bluebell who was licking her paws and cleaning her fur.

"What about the others?" Rowan asked.

"All the colonists will be plotting to be Great Lord Silver now; even those three old fools from the Tanglewood fancy their chances. You should hear them bickering over who would win if they were to fight one another. It's pathetic." He paused. "Can I come with you?" he asked.

"Let me get cleaned up, then I'll ask the others. I can't decide that on my own."

The guards stayed on the Warren Ash-tree, near the hole, long after it was light, hoping to hear sounds from the inside to confirm that their prisoners were still secure. They were puzzled by the updraught that was blowing particles of dust out into the open air, each mote dancing in the sunshine as it was caught by a gentle breeze that eddied round the tree.

Eventually, the bravest one put his head inside, then pulled it out and turned to his companion. "Oh Great Lord Silver," he groaned, "are we in trouble!"

At Blue Pool Base the Greys heard the guards tell of how they had looked in the hollow of the Warren Ash after hearing no sounds from inside during the night, only to find that the prisoners had tunnelled their way out. Malachite conferred with Silica and Obsidian then ordered an immediate tail-chop for the senior guard and a tail-halving for the other. Sentence was carried out gleefully by one of the more recently arrived Greys. Sitka watched in horror. Was this to be the new order of things?

He had waited for an hour, expecting Hickory to reappear. He did not know where his friend was, but he assured the three Lords "that he will be back soon".

"Slack sort of base this," grumbled Malachite. "Never like this in my day."

An hour later Lord Obsidian led a party of colonists to search for the Red males and the missing Grey Leader. They returned to report that a scent trail, and speckles of wood dust particles, led away from the Warren Ash towards the Deepend of the Blue Pool where there were also traces of Hickory's scent.

"The traitor," snarled Malachite. He glowered at Sitka. "I'm taking full command of this precinct. Watch your tail if you know what's good for you," he declared.

Rowan knew they would be pursued soon and he must lead his party to safety, but he must first resolve the question of Hickory coming with them. Hickory was an alien, one of the colonisers who had taken over his land and harassed and persecuted the native Reds. The Greys' whole philosophy had been based on different principles and ideals. The native concept of the guardianship of an area of country was as difficult for a Grey to grasp as "ownership" was to a Red. True he had been teaching native ways to several groups of Greys during the last year, but apart from Hickory and Sitka all the others had moved on west and south, hopefully taking these "native" ideas with them.

The new batch he was teaching had only just started their training and he could not rely on them for support. Sitka might be reliable, but he had never been as enthusiastic nor as friendly as Hickory. Then there were the so-called Three Lords. They were probably harmless enough, far too old and unfit to be a danger.

Rowan remembered that:

> *A delayed Action –*
> *Stultifies. Find the root cause,*
> *Grub it out and Act.*

There was no difficulty in identifying the root cause here; it was that Hickory was a Grey. Could he trust him as one of their party?

Rowan joined the others.

"Hickory," he said, "would you wait over there. I must consult with my companions."

"Of course," said Hickory, "I understand."

When he was safely out of ear-twitch, Rowan spoke. "We can't stay here, so until the situation becomes clearer, we must go into hiding. We will go to the Eyeland in the pool across the Great Heath. Hickory wants to come with us, even though he doesn't know where we are going. Who has views on this?"

He looked at Spindle who spread his paws wide and said, "I've no objections. He's always treated me well. I trust him."

Wood Anemone nodded her assent, as did Rosebay and Willowherb, their heads moving in unison.

Rowan turned to Meadowsweet. "What do you think, Meadowsweet-mate?" he asked.

"I think you should really ask Bluebell," she replied and Rowan looked at her quizzically. Was something going on here that he did not know about? He turned to his daughter.

"Bluebell?"

"Hickory has asked me to be his life-mate," she blurted out. "I've been meaning to talk to you about it, but the time has never been right. I do love him, Rowan-Pa."

A host of queries poured through Rowan's brain, but there was no time to consider them now. One thing was clear though; they all seemed to think that Hickory could be trusted to be on their side in any confrontation.

"We'll have to discuss that later," he said. "I take it then that we are unanimous; Hickory comes with us."

Rowan signalled to Hickory, who came bounding over.

"You can come with us. There are other matters to discuss, but they can wait. Now we will make for a safe place and see what develops. Follow me, all of you."

He headed off towards the Hazel Copse and the Dogleg Field.

The sun was high and the air was warm when they reached the trees whose lower branches spread out over the field. The horses were standing close together, resting in the shade. They were facing in opposite directions, each flicking its tail to keep the flies off the other's head.

"If we go straight across the field and we are followed, our scent will give us away, we'd better lay some false trails."

They were discussing who was to go in which direction and where they were to meet, when Meadowsweet called to Rowan.

"Do you remember Tansy telling us how she came across the harbour on a deer's antler?" she asked. He nodded.

"Well, humans keep horses so that they can travel about the country sitting on their backs. Why can't squirrels ride on horses?"

Rowan looked at the horses below. What would they do if squirrels dropped onto them unexpectedly? But it was a splendidly original idea – worthy of Zander the Great.

"We'll try it," he said. "We won't leave any scent trails that way. That'll fool those Sun-damned Greys." Then, seeing Hickory wince, he added, "Sorry – present company excepted."

The horses had long tails, and manes of coarse hair on the top of their necks and tassels of hair hanging between their eyes.

"Aim for the neck of the chestnut-coloured one. Drop and cling on when I say 'Go'. I expect them to run off when we do that. Then, when I say 'Jump', leap off and follow me."

They all climbed down through the branches until they were just above the horses. They paused there, listening to the gentle snorting noises that the horses made as they communed with one another. Rowan signalled to the squirrels to line up on a branch just above the chestnut.

"Go," he said. "Go now!" and they dropped, each scrabbling for a hold, the unfamiliar smell of horse strong in their nostrils.

The dozing animal reared unexpectedly and Rosebay

and Willowherb, who had not yet got their claws into the security of the mane, slid down the horse's back, unable to grip the short hairs of its summer coat. As they tumbled over its rump, they grasped at the tail and hung on as the frightened animal raced across the field, followed by its puzzled companion, the piebald mare.

Rosebay and Willowherb were swung from side to side as the tail was switched violently in an attempt to dislodge them. When the hedge loomed up in front of it, the chestnut turned, rearing and plunging, its frightened whinnying showing its distress.

"Jump," called Rowan, "Jump now!" and one grey and five red squirrels leapt from the horse's neck for the safety of the hedgerow. Rosebay and Willowherb dropped from its tail and dodging the flying hooves of the black and white mare as it raced by, they scampered for the hedge to join the others.

"That'll break our scent trail," Rowan said, exhilaration in his voice as they stood together, composing themselves after their ride, "Meadowsweet-mate, that was a brilliant idea!"

Chapter 12

Lord Malachite was watching Obsidian and Silica to see how *they* would react to his assumption of command. It was a daring move on his part, he was thinking, appropriate to a born leader. Often the best way – act positively and other lesser squirrels will follow meekly. The more confident you sound the less likely they are to challenge.

Now the lesser squirrels seemed bemused, waiting for his next move. He must keep the initiative; reinforce his position.

Where was Sitka? He was the other one to watch. If that traitor Hickory was off with those native Reds, Sitka might go too. They had both had many moons of that poisonous, corrupting Red influence. Ah, there he was, ready to obey. That was better.

"Right, this is the situation. A group of natives has infiltrated their way into this precinct under the guise of teaching us Silver Squirrels their nasty native ways. We will not tolerate this indignity. The two males we held in the Warren Ash tricked their guards – who have been dealt with in an appropriate way – and escaped. No doubt they have joined their pretty little females. Worst of all, Hickory, rot his name, appears to have joined them. Probably fancies a bit of red-tail. We will hunt them down and dispose of the problem once and for all. Never trust a native with their sneaky, underpaw ways. Follow me."

He led off towards the Little Pool, followed by a posse of Greys, with Sitka behind them and Obsidian and Silica bringing up the rear and grumbling at the effort.

Malachite halted the column before they reached the Deepend area. He was breathing hard.

"We will pause here," he said. "We must not alert the enemy by rushing out and letting them get away."

"Lord Obsidian," Malachite called across. "Take a party and circle round to the east? Lord Silica – do the same to the west? Sitka will go right round and cut off their retreat. When you are in position I will advance from here. Don't let any escape. Kill on capture. Death to all Reds – and all traitors." He scowled a warning at Sitka.

Sitka, with a dozen Greys at his heels, ran from tree to tree to get behind his teachers and erstwhile friends as if to cut off any way of escape. He was surprised that Hickory had abandoned both his own kind and any hope of challenging for the position of Great Lord Silver. Hickory had, at one time, been as keen on this as any Grey male. But what a fool this Malachite was. Still, it was best to go along with him for the time being, he didn't want to lose his tail and there may be a way to help the Reds without compromising his own position.

When Sitka's posse was beyond the Little Pool they picked up the clear scent of Reds, with Hickory's among them, leading away towards the Hazel Copse. The enemy had gone. The trap, if one could call it that, was empty.

Sitka contemplated following the trail at once but decided it would be wiser not to risk the anger of their new self-appointed chief. He turned up-trail and reached the Little Pool as a disappointed Malachite arrived from the other direction.

Sitka reported what he had found.

"Right," said Malachite, "just what I expected. They've sneaked away. That's good news. Now we can have a proper hunt – I always enjoyed those. An exhilarating chase across country, overtake the quarry, surround them, outnumber them, then the kill. Great sport! The quarry probably enjoys it too. Good fun all round. Who said natives are all bad? Follow me."

The Grey force followed Malachite along the scent trail, and through the Hazel Copse to the trees on the edge of the Dogleg Field where the trail came to a dead end. They sniffed around, some going down to the ground where the horse droppings obliterated any more delicate scents, but even when searchers had ventured out into the field beyond the trees there was nothing to indicate which way the quarry had gone.

"Crafty little tree-rats," Malachite declared. "They must have back-tracked. We will rest for a while, then fan out and search either side of the trail. Someone wake me after High-sun."

Rowan kept looking over his shoulder, fearful that their trick with the horses might not have worked and that they would soon hear the sounds of pursuit. He urged his party on, though they were making good time, all being strong and fit, with no very young or old squirrels to slow their progress. He would not be happy until they were safe on his Eyeland in the pool that was named after him – Rowan's Pool. They could hide up there and, if they were found and attacked, they would have the advantage of being able to defend the Eyeland from firm ground while attackers would be wading ashore. All he needed now was a Woodstock.

He scanned every clump of hazel and goat-willow as they followed humans' pathways and old overgrown tramways across the Great Heath. He chose a route to the south of the direct line to his pool; he would overshoot and work back towards it with as many false trails as they could lay. These would help to confuse any possible pursuers.

There were a lot of bushes on which honeysuckle was growing, but nowhere could he see the tight strangling spirals that forced the host plant to grow the bulging twists of wood that trapped the Life-Force and gave the Woodstocks their power. Most bines trailed loosely through the branches or, if they did twist, were too slack to affect the host. Twice he thought they were lucky but, on climbing up, he found that the honeysuckle had won the battle and strangled the life out of the hazel. The Woodstock that had once formed was now just a hollow of dead bark filled with fragments of rotten wood.

In another place they found a rotted Woodstock lying on the ground. The success of the woodbine in killing its host had resulted in both the woodbine and Woodstock collapsing to the ground in a tangled heap.

The squirrels checked briefly when the fresh scent of a fox drifted across their path, inducing Fox-dread.

"Off the ground," Rowan ordered, and they scurried up

the nearest tree, a stunted pine, Hickory staying just behind Bluebell. They were safe here, but they could not stay indefinitely. Rowan asked for two volunteers to join him in a scouting party to establish if the fox was far enough away for them to pass. He hoped they would not have to lose time by back-tracking.

The entire party volunteered and he selected the twins, Rosebay and Willowherb to come with him; it was time these two came more to the fore. They tended to stay behind the others, always whispering to one another. Rowan explained his plan.

They would drop to the ground, then work upwind following the scent. He would lead. The others were to keep him in view but stay well behind so that if he was ambushed they could report back. If this did happen, they were *not* to attempt a rescue; their job would be to inform the others.

At ground level the scent was quite strong and the scouting party moved up the scent-line, with Rowan a long squirrel-leap ahead. He climbed onto a stump and stood up to his full height, his nostrils twitching. The fox was close; probably in that clump of bracken just across the grassy track. He stared at it, every muscle tense and quivering, separating stem from frond with his eyes. The dark mass was heather, he was sure of that. Above it was a brown shape that *might* be an early tinge of autumn colour.

Rowan leapt sideways as the fox sprang. By the time it recovered its balance he was running along the track, leading the fox away from where his companions were waiting in the stunted pine.

Rowan ran, passing several single trees that would have offered him immediate safety, until he came to a clump with a thicket beyond. He leapt for the nearest pine trunk, hearing the snap of the frustrated fox's jaws below him.

He climbed leisurely up to one of the higher branches and watched it prowl about below, then pause, prick up its ears and, after listening for a moment, slip noiselessly away into the furze. Rowan listened too; human voices were just audible. He lay on the branch, the smell of warm resin strong in his nostrils, as two humans, with sticks in their hands and bright blue loads on their backs, passed underneath, heading towards the place where he had left his party.

He ran down the tree trunk to the ground and followed close behind the humans until he was near the tree where the other squirrels were hiding.

Rosebay and Willowherb had reported back, breathlessly.

"Uz zaw a vox jump out at Rowan, him jumped zidewayz."

"Rowan jumped zidewayz when the vox jumped at him."

"The vox mizzed him and him ran away."

"Him ran away when the vox mizzed him."

"The vox wuz chazing him."

"Him wuz being chazed by the vox."

"Slowly, slowly," said Meadowsweet as the sisters told the story, Willowherb as always echoing Rosebay. "He'll be all right. Rowan will have some trick to play on it. Was it a fox or a vixen?"

"Him wuz zleek and vat."

"Vat and zleek him wuz."

"Probably a fox then. Vixens are thin and scraggy at this

time of year. Feeding the cubs wears them down. The scent was almost certainly from a male. You'll remember it now?"

"Yez," the sisters nodded together.

Spindle and Hickory were sitting up, alert. "Humans coming," Spindle said. "Keep out of sight."

Rowan called up when the walkers had passed under the tree.

"Come down quickly and follow me. The fox won't come near the humans, and *they* never watch their tails."

"They don't have tails to watch," said Meadowsweet, brushing whiskers briefly with Rowan.

Chapter 13

On this same fine summer morning, two squirrels were talking together in one of the Ourland trees, much as their mother Marguerite and her brother Rowan had done years before at the Blue Pool. These yearlings were Marguerite and Juniper's son and daughter, Oak and Burdock. Oak was named after his grandfather and Burdock after her great grandmother, both of whom were long Sun-gone and buried together, nourishing the Council Tree in Beech Valley. Their father, Juniper, had died heroically on the Mainland in the battle against the Greys at the Agglestone Rock the year before.

Neither Oak nor Burdock had chosen mates this year, much to Marguerite's disappointment, though each had a drey near to her own.

"If we'd stayed on the Mainland," said Oak the Wary, "we'd both have been on climbabout by now. I've been round Ourland so many times I know every tree and bush. I'm bored – think of something for us to do."

"I must admit that, with food everywhere, and nothing trying to kill us, life is just too Sun-damned easy," Burdock the Thoughtful replied. "We should be grateful to the Sun, but yes – I'm bored too." She was silent for a moment then said, "I know. Let's be News-squirrels!"

"What are News-squirrels?"

"Squirrels who tell the others what is going on. No one hears anything much now. Any news that does get told is by old Post-squirrels with no imagination."

"Surely News-squirrels shouldn't have imagination. They should just report what they see, accurately," Oak said.

"Boring, boring, boring," said Burdock. "News should be exciting, fun, entertaining – like Dandelion's stories."

"But news often isn't exciting," protested Oak, warily.

"It could be if it's told right," replied Burdock. "Come on. Let's be News-squirrels."

"Don't we need permission or something?"

"I don't think so. We'll soon find out if we just do it. Let's find something happening."

They called at the drey of Tansy Stoutheart and the one-eyed Tamarisk Greatleap. They were foraging together with their three dreylings. Greetings were exchanged but it was obvious that nothing newsworthy was going on here. These two, who had lived such dramatic lives on the Mainland, were now happily domesticated.

"We're News-squirrels," said Burdock, "seeking a story. What's new?"

"Nothing much," said Tamarisk, after a moment's hesitation, remembering how, when he was young, he had been prone to blurting out whatever came into his head. As Tamarisk the Tactless he had hurt many feelings and given away secrets which it would have been better to have left unsaid. "What sort of things do you want to know?"

"Anything unusual."

"Chip the Ruddled has got something odd down in the Zwamp," Tamarisk said, looking at Tansy with his one good eye. He knew that Chip still carried a catkin for her and wasn't sure if she didn't do the same for him. "There might be a story there for you."

Chip, absorbed in his Bark-rush, did not see Oak and Burdock until they were close to him.

"It's a good job we're not predators," said Oak.

"Yes," said Chip crossly. "Were you looking for someone?"

"You," said Burdock. "Tamarisk said you had something odd here. We're News-squirrels," she added.

Chip was trying to hide the Bark-rush behind his back. There was a big difference in Marguerite seeing it and these two prying about. They might be her son and daughter and of his age, but they had never been close, despite journeying together the previous year.

"Come on," said Oak to Burdock. "He doesn't want us to see it, whatever it is."

"Not so fast," Burdock replied. "I'm sure that Chip would rather tell all about it, than have us guess and tell wrong things to other squirrels. Wouldn't you Chip?"

"Well," said Chip, hesitantly, "I call it a Bark-rush. You can count on it and work things out."

"Like what?"

"Like how many squirrels there will be on the island if everybody keeps on having dreylings at the rate they are."

"Neither of us have got any," said Oak defensively.

"Hush," said Burdock. "Chip is going to tell us about his bark-rush thing. Why do you call it that?"

"Because it is made from bark and rushes," Chip replied.

"But that's a silly name – how does it work?"

Chip slid the rings back and forth but neither Oak nor Burdock could see what made Chip so proud of it.

"That'll have to be our story," said Burdock. "Chip the Ruddled invents a Bark-rush."

"Do you have to use my tag?" asked Chip.

"Not if you tell us everything," Burdock replied. "Now what were you going to tell us about all those dreylings?"

Marguerite heard the story second or even third paw.

"Chip's Bark-rush invention is going to make all the squirrels have lots of dreylings and soon the island will sink under the weight of them all."

"Chip said that?" Marguerite asked her informer.

"Well, something like that. The News-squirrel – your daughter, Burdock – told my friend only this afternoon and she told me. What should we do?"

"Leave it to me," said Marguerite.

She found Oak and Burdock at their dreys and asked about the "story". Oak told her what Chip had told them about the Bark-rush.

"Did he say that the island would sink under the weight of all the squirrels?"

Oak was silent and Burdock said, "Well, not exactly, but that made a good story."

"That's downright irresponsible," said Marguerite. "You two, of all squirrels, ought to know better."

"Why us?" asked Burdock.

"You're my family."

"So what – does that make us different?" Burdock snapped back.

Oak put a restraining paw on his sister's shoulder but she shook it off.

"I'm fed up with always being your daughter and other squirrels expecting us to behave better than *they* have to. We – I at least – am a News-squirrel and I shall say whatever I like about whoever I want to."

She ran along a branch and leapt into the next tree.

Oak called after her but Burdock snarled over her shoulder, "You can go and get lost for all I care!"

Marguerite sighed and looked upset.

Oak went to her and said, "Marguerite-Ma, I'm sorry that Burdock spoke to you that way, but it's true. It is hard being your family and trying to live up to what you, and other squirrels expect of us. Especially now."

"Why especially now?"

"Things are not right here on Ourland – I'm sure you can see that. There's no danger to keep us alert and wary, as squirrels should be. No excitement. There's masses of food everywhere; our Mainland ideas are not fully accepted by the island squirrels, and the old Royal ways and disciplines you've told us about, don't apply any more. Squirrels just don't know where they are."

Marguerite looked at her son proudly. He had summed up exactly what she had been feeling. She let him carry on.

"By all accounts, Just Poplar made a good leader when

you were not here on Ourland. He always tries to be fair and live up to his 'Just' tag, but he feels over-awed by you.''

"*Me?*" said Marguerite incredulously. "*Me?*"

"Yes, you, Marguerite-Ma. Every squirrel can see that you are far cleverer than he is. He's afraid that you will disagree with his decisions.''

"I would never dream of interfering.'' Marguerite felt herself to be on the defensive. "I never would.''

"I know that, but it makes him uneasy and indecisive. Remember he is used to one strong squirrel being in charge. A King in fact.''

"That's all over and done with,'' said Marguerite. "It was Just Poplar himself who gave up being King.''

"I know, but there are a few squirrels – more than a few – who would like *you* to be Queen.''

"Me? Queen of Ourland? Out of the question. I thought they all called me Miss Hoity-Toity.''

"Only a few of the younger ones. Don't take any notice of them – they speak from under their tails.''

"What do *you* think?'' Marguerite sat back, tail low, awaiting her son's verdict.

Oak thought for a moment, then replied, "It's difficult for me. If you were Queen then I would be Next-King and I'm not sure if I want that. There is no doubt that you are the cleverest squirrel on the island, bar none.''

Marguerite's tail rose a little.

"Squirrels say Chip is clever, and he is, but he hasn't got your experience, nor wisdom, nor your ability to find the truth buried beneath the facts.''

Marguerite's tail rose higher.

"I think you would make a good Queen, or Leader, call it

95

what you will, and I think all the squirrels would accept you, though some of the ex-zervantz might not be too keen on the idea of being zervantz again."

"They needn't be. Just because there was a Queen, or a King, there needn't be zervantz!"

"True, but it would take some time to convince them. Nothing should be done hastily," said Oak the Wary. "Now, what *is* the truth in what Chip told Burdock and me about Ourland being overrun with squirrels?"

Chapter 14

Lord Malachite was woken from a dream in which he was taking his place in the Oval drey as the new Great Lord Silver. The trees around were full of respectful Silver squirrels chanting his praises as he climbed to his rightful position. Then some minion was shaking his shoulder.

"Wake up sir, it's past High-sun."

"How dare you," he snapped.

"I'm sorry, sir. You said to wake you."

Malachite scratched at an invisible flea. "Yes, so I did, so I did. Anything to report."

"No, sir. We've been waiting for you."

"Quite right, quite right. We must find where the quarry backtracked. Everybody search. Leave no trees unsniffed."

Miles away across the Great Heath, the human walkers had reached the road passing to the west of Rowan's Pool and turned along it towards Screech Hill. In the hedges on either side of the road were many trees and bushes with honeysuckle growing up them; the sweet scent of the yellow trumpet-shaped flowers drowning the tarry smell from the hot surface of the road.

The squirrels watched the humans walk away out of their sight, confident that the fox was no longer a threat, but listening for the hum of the travelling boxes that humans used on these roadways. Whenever the road was clear, they again searched for a suitable Woodstock, hiding in the hedges when vehicles came by.

It was Wood Anemone who found one, a bulky twist on a hazel sapling, with the honeysuckle bine almost buried in the wood that had grown out and around it. Rowan sensed its power; running his paws over the bark, his whiskers vibrating with the hidden force trapped in the fibres.

"This is a strong one," he said, then started to gnaw at the stem above the twisted bulge.

In a short time he had cut the sapling through above and below the twist, and had bitten away the bitter bine itself, letting the Woodstock fall into the hedge. From there they dragged it out onto the grass verge and across the road towards Rowan's Pool.

"Uz wouldn't like to have to take thiz wun var," said Spindle, remembering the long journey of the previous year. "What diztanze iz yewr pool from here?"

"Not far, just through those chestnut and pine trees."

Even so, it was twilight when they dragged the Woodstock through the trees and reached the bank that surrounded the pool. They looked down on the Eyeland that they hoped would offer safety for them all once they had swum across to it.

A tree had been blown down, probably in the Great Storm, and was lying in the water – making a bridge from the Mainland!

Rowan said something under his breath but perhaps a

little too loudly. Meadowsweet looked at him, her eyes wide. "Rowan!" she said.

Rosebay and Willowherb giggled and nudged one another. Hickory looked surprised and glanced at Bluebell.

"Stay here at the top of the bank and keep alert," Rowan said. "Spindle and I will go and investigate."

The two males crossed the water using the fallen tree, and dropped from it onto the tufty grass and lichen that covered the ground. There was no scent of danger there, nor in the three trees. The Eyeland seemed to Spindle to be much smaller than when he had seen it two years before, It was little more than a squirrel leap from one side to the other.

"What now?" he asked.

"This'll have to do for tonight," Rowan replied. "In the morning we'll find a safer place. At least here we can only be attacked from one direction. Let's get the Woodstock over here."

The twisted stick was rolled down the bank and carefully dragged across the tree trunk to the Eyeland as the moon rose in the east, throwing an eerie light on the busy squirrels. Rowan was trying to remember the shapes that Marguerite had cut on earlier weapons and wished now that he had taken more notice when she had tried to teach him numbers.

There was a **1** then a **2**. After that was a **4**, or was it a **3**?

"Who remembers the numbers that go on a Woodstock?" he asked, turning expectantly to Meadowsweet, who spread her paws.

"Sorry, Rowan-mate," she said.

"Uz doez," said Wood Anemone. "Uz doezn't know what they iz called, but uz knowz the zhapz well 'nuff. Uz uzed to polizh the old Woodztock when Marguerite wuz not there. Uz liked to zee it all clean and tidy-like."

Rowan set Rosebay and Willowherb to guard the bridge and sent Bluebell up the tallest tree to listen for any sounds of approaching danger. The others all worked at stripping off the bark and biting the magic numbers deep into the hazel wood – 1 Z 3 4 5 6 7 10 X.

Hickory watched in fascination, taking his turn in the cutting and asking questions about the shapes of the numbers.

There was some argument about the X. Rowan said it was Marguerite's special mark and was therefore not needed, but the others, especially Wood Anemone, felt it was important. "It worked vor uz with that X there; it may not work without it," she argued, and so the X was cut, leaving space for the numbers which activated the force and controlled its power and range.

Bats circled between the trees and flittered away down the length of the pool, snatching at moths and other night flying insects, their shrill cries sharp in the still air. A night-jar churred from a branch across the water reminding Rowan of the year he had lived on the Eyeland alone.

Whilst they had been dragging the Woodstock to the pool a young Grey was once more waking Malachite.

"Lord Malachite, sir. We've found the trail. It's on the other side of the field. It crosses the roadway and goes onto the Great Heath."

Malachite looked at the angle of the sun. Was it really

that late? He must have been dozing again. The quarry would have a good start. Too late to follow now. They would set out at first light and allow a full day for the hunt. In the meantime he had some other business that must be seen to.

"Everybody back to base," he ordered. "Get a good night's rest. Where are the Lords Silica and Obsidian?"

"They retired early, sir. They went back to their dreytels."

In the North-east Wood, Silica and Obsidian were discussing Malachite's behaviour.

"He's fallen off his stump!" said Silica. "Can't he see that things have changed. I'm surprised that the other Silvers follow him so readily."

"I think they're thrown, with Hickory leaving like that. Fancy a Silver running off after Red-tail, assuming that's what's behind it."

"Dangerous to assume. What was it that Red female told us?"

> *Squirrels who don't check*
> *May assume a fox's mouth*
> *To be a safe den.*

"Don't start quoting their Kernels at me," Lord Obsidian growled. "You'll be wanting *me* to behave like a little native next."

They were silent for a while, each busy with their thoughts. Finally Silica spoke.

"Do you think we've been out of action too long?" he

asked. "The whole world seems to be upside-down now. I'm tempted to slip back to the Tanglewood and live the quiet life. Be lonely on my own, though. Would you come with me?"

Then, before he had an answer, he added, "Obsidian-Friend, as the Red ones put it."

"Sun-dammit I will – as the Red ones would put it. Let's slip away before the hordes come back – Silica-Friend."

"What about Malachite?"

"Him! He's obsessed with the idea of becoming Great Lord Silver. When he's got over that and finds us gone, no doubt he'll follow us. Come on, I've had enough of this."

Lord Malachite returned to New Massachusetts with Sitka, explaining to him why he had put off following the fugitives until the next day. "We'll all be fresh then, have a good day's hunting. Run those natives down by High-sun I'm sure. And the traitor! You can have the honour of killing him. I'll remember that when I'm in high places. You'll need to show which side you're on since you've been mixed up in this native business for so long. See you at first light. What was your name again?"

The moon was high when Malachite slipped out of his dreytel and went silently through the branches towards Silica's. It was good that Obsidian's dreytel was some distance beyond that. This was worthy of Zander the Great: original thinking, the element of surprise, ruthlessness – good leadership qualities those. If he could get Silica and Obsidian while they were asleep, he could kill them before they knew what was happening. Bite the throat and hold on – it should only take a minute or two to get those rivals out of contention. But he would have to do it without waking the other Silvers.

At Silica's dreytel he paused and listened. There was no sound of breathing. A thought flashed across his mind. What if Silica had planned the same thing? Maybe Silica had already killed Obsidian and was now on his way to kill him. No – he would have seen or heard him.

Malachite went and listened outside Obsidian's dreytel. Silence again.

He thought up some pretext about changing the start time for the hunt, and shook the twigs of the sleeping place, then put his head inside. It too was empty.

Perhaps they were out together, looking for him! He imagined sharp teeth biting into his neck; looked around fearfully in the spooky moonlight, then sought an unused dreytel, well away from his own, and spent a restless night there, only dozing off when the moon had set.

"Lord Malachite, sir. It's dawn, sir. We had a job to find you, sir. It's all right, sir. It's only me, sir. Are you all right, sir?"

Malachite looked bleary-eyed at the youngster, one of the new arrivals.

"Yes, yes. Of course I am. What was your name again?"

As dawn lightened the sky over the little island in the pool, the Woodstock was as complete as Rowan and Spindle could make it. They relieved the guards on the bridge and sent all the others up the trees to sleep. Wood Anemone gave the gleaming twisted wood one last rub with a piece of soft moss.

"Watch that I don't fall asleep, Spindle-Friend," Rowan said.

"Yew'd better do the zame for uz," the ex-zervant replied.

Rowan watched as a heron flapped slowly over the pool before starting a long glide down to the shallow water at the far end; the trueness of its flight indicating that there was no apparent danger from that direction.

Chapter 15

Hickory had come with Bluebell at mid morning to relieve Rowan and Spindle at the bridge.

"Call me if you see anything suspicious. I'll sleep near the Woodstock in case we need to use it," Rowan told them.

Though desperately tired, sleep did not come easily. From where he lay in a tussock of grass he could see Hickory and Bluebell sitting on the peeling bark of the bridge, saying things he could not hear. It was clear from the way they sat so close together how they felt about one another. How had he missed this before?

What would happen if they mated, as they clearly planned to do? Remembering Bluebell's namesake and the Greys of the Silver Tide, he knew that a mating must be physically possible. But would the Sun bless the union with dreylings and, if it did, what would they be like? Would they be grey or red, or a patchy mixture, like the horse in the Dogleg Field? Whatever colour they were, they would be his grandchildren and he would love them.

Rowan finally dropped off to sleep, dreaming of being a grandfather and playing under a peaceful sun with a tumbling mass of piebald dreylings.

Malachite asked the assembled Greys if anyone had seen the other two Lords. None had, neither that day nor the previous evening. He selected two young males and briefed them privately.

"I've got a special and secret mission for you," he said in a conspiratorial voice. "I have chosen you out of all the others to follow Lord Silica and Lord Obsidian and report back to me exactly what they are doing. Don't let them see you, and tell no one but me what you find out." He put a claw to his lips. "No one but me. Understand?"

The youngsters nodded, proud to have been selected, though they were disappointed to be missing the hunt.

"Wait until we have gone, then follow your noses. I will expect a report tonight. If we are not here – follow our trail."

He turned back to address the others, surprised and pleased to see how many had turned out for the chase. Not only were most of those who had been at Rowan's current training present, but yet another new batch of colonists had just arrived and they were eager to join in.

The squirrels crossed the Dogleg Field in a grey mass and flowed over the road in the early light. Scouts had been sent ahead to find the scent and they guided the hunters through the furze, heather and fern of the Great Heath.

By High-sun the scouts had reported that the quarry were trapped on an island in a pool, with a tree-trunk bridge leading to it.

"I don't think they have seen us," Malachite was told by the scout leader. "Most of them are asleep, but the traitor, Hickory, and a Red female are on guard."

"Rot his tail," said Malachite to Sitka. "How do you fancy single combat on the bridge. That should be good sport."

Sitka looked apprehensive. "He was my friend," he said.

"Not now, surely – he's a proven traitor. You kill him, then we'll deal with the natives."

"Let's see exactly what the situation is first," said Sitka. "The Red ones taught us a saying."

In a strange country,
Be careful. Time spent looking
Is seldom wasted.

"Humph," said Malachite, but sent out parties of squirrels to surround the pool, in case the quarry tried to escape by swimming, then approached the edge of the bank where they could all look down onto the island.

Hickory was sitting on the bridge with Bluebell at his side, both facing the mainland. He felt her body stiffen.

"Don't look at once," she whispered, "but I am sure there are squirrels up there on the bank, watching us."

"Red or Silver?" Hickery whispered back.

"Grey," she said.

"Go as casually as you can and wake your father. Tell him what you've seen. I'll stay here."

Bluebell stretched and went slowly back along the fallen trunk and relieved herself behind a clump of rushes, conscious as she did so, that, though out of sight of her party, she was in full view of "lots" of enemy Greys.

Then she went over to where her father lay at the foot of

one of the pines and said, "Rowan-Pa. Wake up, the Greys are here. Slowly now, they don't know we have seen them."

"Climb the tree and tell the others," he said calmly. "I'll cover the bridge with the Woodstock."

"My Hickory is down there, call him back if you have to use it, don't curl *his* whiskers,'" Bluebell told her father, then slowly climbed the tree, as though she was going up to sleep there.

Hickory was watching the top of the bank. Bluebell had been right, there were lots of Silvers there. He turned his head – there were more to be seen on the opposite bank, all just sitting and watching. The fur on the back of his neck rose slowly and his tail started to swish from side to side, betraying his fear.

He saw a Silver come down the bank towards him, tail low, in the "Parley" position. It was Sitka.

Hickory sat still as he approached.

"Hickory-Friend," Sitka said quietly. "That old fool Malachite wants me to challenge you to single combat. What should I do?"

"Look fierce," said Hickory, "and talk."

Sitka raised his tail, arched his back, stamped his feet on the bridge and churred the Challenge. Hickory did the same.

"Hickory, come back here," Rowan called, "clear of the bridge."

Hickory signalled an unmistakable "leave me alone" with his tail, while still facing Sitka.

"What do you want to do?" he hissed at Sitka.

"Find a mate, live in peace and bring up a family under the Sun – that Great Lord Silver business is a sham. I can see that now," Sitka hissed back.

"You won't do that with Malachite in charge. His head is full of punkwood. Come and join us."

"I can't do that, you're outnumbered many times. You'll all be zapped by nightfall."

"We've got a Woodstock," hissed Hickory. "I don't think old Punkhead knows what that is. Come and join us."

"Get on with it, damn you both," Malachite's voice came from the bank behind Sitka. "Or are you rabbits?"

They ignored the insult and went on with the charade.

"Are you a Sun-squirrel?" Hickory asked.

"Yes."

"You never told me."

"You never asked. Are you?"

"Yes."

"You never told me."

"You never asked."

A small pine cone splashed in the water beside them as a gruff voice called down, "Get on with it."

"I'll go and ask Malachite to give you all safe passage," Sitka said, while going through the motions of stamping and arching his back again.

Hickory made the same movements, advancing towards Sitka who moved backwards.

"Not a chance, the old fool is using this, and you, as a step towards the Oval Drey. He fancies himself as Great Lord Silver."

Hickory moved backwards to allow Sitka to make a forward feint.

"I've got to give it a try. We Sun-squirrels have to do what we think is right."

Hickory stood to his full height, saluted with his right

paw diagonally across his chest. Sitka, facing him, did the same then they embraced briefly as a shower of cones flew around them, bouncing off the bridge and dropping into the water.

Sitka turned and, tail high, went up the bank to where Lord Malachite sat glowering down at him. Sitka lowered his tail, remembering the Request Kernel he had been taught by Rowan, though forgetting for the moment that Malachite would not know this.

A submissive stance
And a request, presumes help –
Give it if you can.

"Lord Malachite. These are good squirrels, all friends of mine, please let them pass safely."

"They are natives and traitors, as you are showing yourself to be. A cowardly one at that. Your body will hang in a tree as an example to others. Zap him!" he ordered and a group of Greys leapt on to Sitka, biting and scratching.

The Reds on the island, and Hickory on the bridge, watched, unable to see clearly what was happening in the mêlée at the top of the bank. Then they saw a limp grey body being hauled up a pine trunk and dragged out along a branch where it was suspended, with its neck jammed in a fork. The tail moved slowly in a slight breeze.

Hickory saluted again.

"Come back here, Hickory-Friend," Rowan called, and the Grey turned and slowly climbed the gentle slope of the island to where the Reds were clustered around the Woodstock. Bluebell moved over to crouch beside him.

"They will attack soon," said Rowan, "but we are ready for them."

Chapter 16

Malachite looked down at the island and was about to order "Attack". He had decided to stay up on the bank and direct from there, rather than get involved himself. "Only fair to give these youngsters a chance to prove themselves," he was telling himself. "Wouldn't do to get injured myself when I am about to make the journey to Woburn and challenge the Great Lord Silver. Must keep myself fit for that."

There was something about the way the natives on the island were clustered together. Not in terror or in panic as he would have expected, but confidently, as though they knew something he didn't. Were there reinforcements on the way? Instinctively, he glanced over his shoulder, then realised that there were no other natives in the area. It couldn't be that.

The nearby Silvers were all looking to him for leadership, waiting for the order to pour across the bridge and dispose of the quarry. He looked again at the natives. There was something on the ground in front of them. He rubbed his eyes; just lately he found he could not see distant things as clearly as he used to.

"What's that in front of them?" he barked at a youngster near him.

"It's a stick, sir. A sort of knobbly one."

"What's it for?"

"I don't know, sir. It might be some kind of totem, these natives do have some funny customs."

"There's a prime territory for any squirrel who can bring it to me – spread the word. What's your name?"

"Monterey, sir, same as the new Great Lord Silver, sir."

"Well, Monterey, how do you fancy living up to that name. Go and get that knobbly stick. If you bring it to me you get a choice of territories. Off you go now – go on."

Monterey braced himself, rushed down the bank and leapt onto the bridge. He saw one of the natives scratch at the knobbly stick and then felt as if he had been hit by an invisible whirlwind. His head swam, lights flashed in his eyes and, losing his balance he fell from the bridge into the water. The shock cleared his head a little and he struggled for the bank, splashing clumsily. The squirrels who helped him ashore saw that his whiskers were coiled into tight little curls. He begged them to bite them off before he could report back to Malachite.

"It works," Rowan said, "we must have got those numbers right." He looked at the sun.

"About four hours to sunset, I wonder if they will try again?"

Lord Malachite, who had never seen a Woodstock in action before, was interrogating Monterey.

"A wave hit you? I didn't see any wave, you've lost your

brains as well as your whiskers. Everybody on this side get ready for a mass charge. Ready now. CHARGE."

Malachite watched a flood of squirrels pour down the bank towards the bridge. As the first reached the fallen trunk it rolled sideways, clawing at its face, as did the next and the next. The other squirrels turned and scrambled up the bank leaving the three behind.

Malachite watched in astonishment. This was more than a totem that the Reds had. It was an amazingly powerful weapon. It was as well that he had been wise enough to stay up on the bank. Wouldn't do for his battle group to lose their Commander.

"Bring up the injured," he ordered.

The Reds watched a small party of Greys come cautiously down the bank, their tails low, and help the three with the curled whiskers climb back up.

"What now?" Hickory asked.

"Wait and watch," said Rowan.

Unknown Danger near
Lie high, wait, watch and look out.
Trust in the Sun's light.

"The danger's not unknown," said Hickory.

"Kernels don't always fit exactly, but the message is clear. Keep alert – Trust in the Sun."

Meadowsweet asked if she should organise the building of dreys in the trees.

Rowan looked up at the three trunks, then across at the mainland.

"It goes contrary to squirrel nature, but I think we should make a ground-drey. There's no fox-danger here at present and if we are on the ground and all together, we can react faster to anything the Greys do."

With one watching the bridge and another scanning the bank across the water behind them, the other Reds collected fallen twigs, biting off and dropping more dead ones from the trees. With these they built a hollow mound, large enough to take them all. The females used their skills with grass and moss to make a warm lining.

Dusk was falling and there was no sign of another attack. Rowan sat outside the ground-drey, thinking, his paw on the Woodstock. Across the narrow strip of water he could see Sitka's body hanging, the tail moving eerily whenever the evening breeze eddied among the trees. Another Sun-squirrel gone. At least he had died standing up for what he believed in.

Rowan remembered how Sitka and Hickory had helped with the classes for the colonists passing through, allocating them to those skimpy dreytels. Then organising the new-comers so that they all absorbed the messages of the Kernels and were at least partly Sun-worthy before they moved on to take up Territories. He could not, even now, get used to the idea of squirrels owning things, especially woods.

What had happened to all those Greys he had taught? They had left after each course was complete, vowing friendship with their teachers and with each other, brushing whiskers and embracing, and arranging reunions that Rowan had ruefully thought were unlikely ever to take place once the harshness of survival in a hostile world overtook those who had just graduated.

Why were these Greys now persecuting them? Then he realised that they were only fresh-squirrels, newly arrived, and at most had only a few lessons. How easily they had accepted the Three Lords. Those old fools would not have been able to influence a more experienced class.

Rowan's stomach rumbled and he looked around for food.

There were some fallen cones lying under the trees; there might be a seed or two in those. He looked up at the pines. There were clusters of cones silhouetted against the sky but they would not feed eight squirrels for long. Nothing much on the ground, no fungus; some lichen, but that had little food value, and some tufts of grass which might have done if they were rabbits but was not much use to squirrels. Food was going to be a problem if they had to stay here for long.

He called the others out of the drey and explained the food situation, watching the bank and the bridge as he did so.

"It is unlikely that the Greys will attack again until dawn, they don't care for the darkness any more than we do. But we must stay on guard. You will all be hungry and we don't know how long we must stay here. Eat what you can find tonight, share it out equally and we will think what to do for more in the morning."

Rowan was feeling very tired. He tried to hide a yawn, then said, "Spindle, will you allocate guard duties? One hour periods – two squirrels at a time. Take over now. I am exhausted and must sleep."

He went into the ground-drey, curled up and slept until dawn. Spindle had deliberately omitted him from the roster.

Spindle and Hickory were on duty at midnight, listening to the night sounds and watching for movement. The moon had set and the stars were bright above them. Spindle pointed out the North Star.

'Zee those zeven ztarz there. Uz callz thoze the Great Zquirrel. Thoze are hiz two front pawz. Follow a line up from thoze and that next ztar iz the Ztar that iz alwayz in the North.''

There was a rustling on the bank across the water. Hickory crept down to the bridge to investigate, tense and ready to scamper back if danger was too close. A cone arched through the sky and landed in the water beside him. They *were* being watched. He retreated up the bank as a shower of tiny specks of light shot across the sky and were gone before either squirrel could focus on them.

"Thoze iz zhooting ztarz," Spindle told Hickory.

A little later they woke Bluebell and the twins, taking care not to disturb Rowan. They briefed the females and stayed with them until they were sure that their eyes had adjusted to the darkness and they were fully alert.

"Wake us all if anything seems to be happening," Hickory said. "It's Wood Anemone and Meadowsweet's turn next – wake them in an hour." He brushed whiskers with Bluebell, and Spindle did the same with his daughters. "Yew keep alert, now. Don't let them zurprize yew."

Spindle and Hickory wriggled into the ground-drey and slept.

Chapter 17

Wakened by the light filtering through the sides of the ground-drey, Rowan poked his head out, looked round at the dew-laden grass and drew a deep breath. The smell was familiar to him; the year he had once spent living on this Eyeland, as he had called it then, was still strong in his memory. That was before the tree fell, bridging the water. In those days he had swum back and forth to the Mainland.

Now, he could see Hickory's back down near the bridge and when he turned round he saw Spindle gathering pine needles and throwing them onto the top of the drey. He went and faced him.

"Why didn't you call me – I've missed my guard duties."

"Yew wuz all burned out, Rowan-Friend. Yew will be able to lead uz better now yew iz rezded."

"Thank you, Spindle-Friend, but I should *always* take my proper turn," he said.

The day wore on with no sign of aggression from the Greys. At first the Reds could see them moving about on the top of the bank and in the trees on the Mainland. They waited apprehensively for another attack until Bluebell said,

"Rowan-Pa, I know there are no Kernels to guide us in war, because we have always been peace-loving squirrels, but if there were, I am sure that they would tell us to take the initiative. I hate sitting here waiting for something to happen. There is the one that says:

Your prayers alone
Will not do. The Sun will help
Those who help themselves.

"I know we've all been praying, but surely there is something we can do?"

Rowan nodded, thought for a moment then crept backwards to where the Woodstock lay on the grass. He turned it slowly towards a Grey who was peering at them through the branches opposite, and scratched a 4 on the smooth wood. The Grey dropped to the ground stunned, then, rubbing his whiskers, climbed slowly up the bank to disappear over the top.

The next Grey to show his face met with the same fate. Three more suffered in the same way before they realised that the Red's weapon had a long reach.

Malachite saw the first Grey fall and kept behind his tree-trunk out of sight of the island. The victim was sent for and came, reeling and stumbling, to the foot of the tree to explain what had happened and how he felt.

"Bite off his whiskers," Malachite commanded. "Light duties for three days."

When the third Grey came before him with tightly curled whiskers, Lord Malachite was angry.

"Can't you see what happens when they point that totem thing at you. Keep your heads down, all of you. They've got no food over there; we'll starve them out. Damned unsporting lot, rot their tails. Watch through the grass or from behind leaves, don't let them see you. Back to your positions – now!"

The two youngsters found Malachite behind his tree when they came to report on the Lords Obsidian and Silica.

"They are in a wood on a knoll which is covered in fallen trees," he was told, and he soon established that the two Lords were back in their old dreys in the Tanglewood.

"You have done well," he told the messengers. "Now keep your heads down and find food. Tell no one else." He put a claw to his lips and winked.

Rowan was quite sorry when there were no more heads to discharge the Woodstock at, but knew that he ought to conserve it. The power it held was not infinite and there was no way of knowing how near it was to exhaustion.

The early evening sun shone gently and the Reds sat in a cluster, each facing a different way, watching the bridge and the banks of the pool across the water. No movement was to be seen anywhere.

"Huz them gone away?" Rosebay asked, echoed by Willowherb, "Gone away, huz them?"

"I don't think so," Meadowsweet said. "We can't be sure, better to wait. It may be a trap. My mother would tell a story at times like this. Anyone want to hear about Acorn and the swan's feathers?"

Squirrels never say no to a story but Rowan cautioned them to stay alert while they listened.

Meadowsweet began. "Once upon a time, there were only two squirrels in the world, Acorn and his lovely life-mate Primrose.

"On the day I am going to tell you about, Primrose was relining their drey with new, sweet-smelling moss, and Acorn was walking by a river, thinking. He was thinking how beautiful everything was and what lucky squirrels they were to have such a wonderful world to live in. There were so many things to see and find out.

"He had seen how the seeds grew when the spring sunshine warmed the ground, and he had seen how the autumn sunshine ripened all the fruit and the nuts so that they could be stored ready for eating in the winter.

"Thinking of the winter days, when cold winds blew and snow covered the ground, he began to believe that he could have arranged things better if he had been the Sun. Why have winters at all? Life would be much easier if there were only springs, summers and autumns. In fact, why have summers? It was often too hot in summer to be comfortable.

This is a brilliant idea, he thought.

"He was about to rush back and tell Primrose, when he remembered that she would probably find some good reason for there to be summers and winters. She often spoilt his best ideas by being practical. This was far too good an idea to be spoilt by practicalities. He walked on, enjoying his plans for a year with only springs and autumns. He was not seeing all the good things around him now – he was thinking of a way to tell the Sun that it had got it all wrong.

"Now, as often happens when you think hard enough, and want a thing enough, something will turn up to help you towards getting it.

"This happened to Acorn. There on the river bank were feathers. These had been moulted by the First Swan in the World when the summer heat had told it to shed its old feathers and grow new strong, clean ones for the next year. The swan had taken most of the soft, downy ones to line its nest and keep its eggs warm, but on the bank were the stiff white quills from its wings.

" 'If I could fly like a swan,' Acorn said to himself, 'I would fly up to the Sun and tell it what a mistake it had made creating winters and summers, when all we squirrels need are springs and autumns.'

"Acorn picked up the two longest feathers and held them out, waving them up and down, pretending to be a swan. He would go and tell the Sun. He would. He would. He closed his eyes and flapped as hard as he could.

"When he opened his eyes again, the ground was far below him and he could see the river winding backwards and forwards, looking like a snake does from high on a tree.

"He was so surprised that he forgot to keep his paws, which were holding the feathers, moving up and down and he was falling towards the river. He started to flap the feathers again even faster than before.

"The Sun had been watching all this, smiling warmly to see that one of its little creatures was beginning to think for himself, but had not yet come to rely on the wisdom that it had given to the females.

"The sun decided to teach Acorn a gentle lesson. By now he was flying out over the sea so the Sun decided to drop

Acorn into the water and let him swim to the shore because, as you all know, squirrels, excepting my Rowan, don't like swimming. He loves it and used to swim a lot when he lived all alone on this Eyeland two years ago."

Meadowsweet smiled at her life-mate who was watching the far bank.

"Where was I? Oh yes. The Sun had decided to drop Acorn into the sea as a lesson. The Sun never acts directly in these things, it needs to seem impartial and uncaring, but if you look very closely at things you will see that in some way it influences and directs everything we do. It will arrange things to achieve what it wants. So the Sun made a swallow swoop close beneath Acorn, brushing under his forearm with its wing-tip as it flew by chasing flies. Acorn was so ticklish that he let go of one of the feathers and started to fall. The feather floated away out of his reach, twisting and spinning like a sycamore seed.

"Acorn clung onto the other feather as he fell. He could see that he was going to splash into the sea and would have to swim all the way to the shore – and he did not like the thought of that!

"Now, males often think quickly in emergencies like this, and he did still have *one* feather. He reached up and caught the tip with his free paw and found that he was not falling quite as fast. Then he found that, by twisting the feather, he could go in any direction he liked. He swung round to glide towards the land, intending to come down without even getting his feet wet.

"The Sun was watching this clever little squirrel outwit it, and thought that would never do. So it made an updraught where the wind blew against the cliff; we used to watch the butterflies tossing about in this when we lived near the sea.

"The Sun let Acorn float up again on the rising air, but he soon learned how to twist the feather to take advantage of the updraught and began to glide in towards the soft cliff-top grass. He was starting to think that he had again outwitted the Sun. Clever Acorn, he was thinking.

"The Sun though, was playing with him, and as Acorn had chosen a good place to land and was steering towards it, the Sun reached down a gigantic paw and scooped out a hollow just ahead of him. The hollow was right on the edge of the sea and water rushed in through the gap, foaming and bubbling and soaking Acorn who had to swim ashore – just as the Sun had planned all along.

"When Dandelion told me this story, she said the hollow cove is still there, full of the sea."

"What happened to the scoop of land, Meadowsweet-Ma?" asked Bluebell.

"The Sun looked at it and thought, Where could I have another hill? and seeing that the Great Heath was perhaps just a little too big, dropped it on the south side of that.

"If you climb the tree behind you and look that way you can see it. It's where the barn owls live – Screech Hill."

On Screech Hill itself, Sumac was worried. Word had just reached him on the colonists' woodbine, that a party of Reds were being hunted to the death, over near the Blue Pool.

The only Reds he knew of there were the Teachers – Rowan, Meadowsweet, Spindle and Wood Anemone, with their youngsters. Surely no one was hunting *them*? They were doing a tremendous and worthy job, teaching all the Silvers how to live successfully and peacefully in New America. They were wonderful squirrels and had taught him to be a Sun-squirrel, though it was not something one spoke about too openly. One day, when there was a Sun-squirrel in the Oval Drey perhaps, but not now.

If it *was* his friends and teachers who were being hunted, he ought to be doing something to help them. He told his life-mate Tumbleweed, that he had to be away for a few days and slipped off towards the Blue Pool without further explanation. She still harboured some of the old prejudices, even though she had been taught in the same class as he had. She was not yet ready to become a Sun-squirrel.

Skirting round the edge of the Tanglewood he caught the scent of Obsidian and Silica and crept up on them cautiously, then seeing their apparent age and condition, called to them.

"Do you know anything about some natives being chased?" he asked.

"Who are you?" Silica called back.

"A friend of the Teachers. Is it them?"

"Yes," said Obsidian, but before he could say more, Sumac was off in a flash of grey fur, heading for the Blue Pool.

He ran as fast as he could across the Great Heath and through the woods to New Massachusetts, hardly pausing for breath even when he reached the pool itself. Human visitors looked up as the frantic grey squirrel passed overhead on its way to the North-east Wood.

Here everything was eerily silent. The dreytels were unoccupied and the whole wood empty of any squirrel activity. Sumac snuffled around among the confusing scents, then followed the strongest towards the Dogleg Field.

Chapter 18

Marguerite knew that things were now seriously wrong on Ourland. Instead of peace and prosperity bringing pleasure and happiness to the island, the virtually unlimited leisure time was undermining, if not destroying, the whole culture of the squirrels.

She had retired to one of the palm trees in the sheltered valley to think. Few humans came here and very few squirrels. Not that she disliked humans, they had never threatened her, but she just could not understand them.

They still celebrated their Sun-days every seventh day which seemed rather too often to her. The squirrels' Sun-days were the Longest Day and the Longest Night, the Coming of Spring and the Harvest Safely In. However, the humans did seem to have special Sun-days for the last three of these, as Marguerite, who loved to listen to the humans singing in the island church, had noticed extra activity at those times.

The squirrels' Longest Day celebrations had not gone well that summer. There had been plenty of youngsters romping and playing, but very few of the older generation came along to organise the fun and chases, or to tell stories.

Dandelion had told one of Marguerite's favourite tales about the squirrel who was beaten and then saved by humans, but the youngsters had been inattentive and fidgety.

Marguerite recalled how *she* had always listened in silence when she had been young but this year . . .

Dandelion had started as always, "Once upon a time . . ."

". . . A squirrel went down from Bloxworth to Wolvesbarrow. Some boys, as humans call their young males, set upon this squirrel and threw stones at him. They chased him with sticks, beating and hitting him until he saw the sky go black and blood ran from his nose. Then the boys kicked the poor thing into the grass on the side of a roadway and ran off, laughing.

"All day the squirrel lay there, bothered by flies and afraid that a fox or dog might come and kill and eat him, but he was too stiff and sore and sick to move.

"Several times squirrels passed in the trees overhead and saw the injured one lying below. The first squirrel was in a hurry and pretended not to see him.

"The second one did not want to get involved. It was none of her business, and, anyway, it was the injured squirrel's own fault if he had got himself into trouble.

"The third came down the tree and went a little closer to look. When he saw that the squirrel was a stranger he passed by on the other side.

"Then a human came, saw the creature lying in the grass and took pity on him. He took it to a clean white place where he lived with other sick animals. Here other humans nursed him back to health and then released him where he had been found.

"That injured squirrel was my dear grandfather, and he often told this story as a warning that you must not expect all of one kind to behave in the same way – especially humans.

"My grandfather could never understand how humans could care so much for their pet dogs and cats and for sick creatures, then go out and kill free animals and birds just to have fun."

Dandelion had looked around expecting to see the nods and tail-flicks of appreciation that usually followed her story-telling and was upset when Sycamore said, "You're always going on at us with your silly stories. I'm off." He turned his tail on Dandelion and leapt for a tree trunk, displaying insolence in his every movement. Other youngsters had followed him.

What could be done, Marguerite wondered. Every generation thinks the older ones are stick-on-the-grounds. She could remember having such thoughts herself, but her year-mates wouldn't have dared behave like that. Perhaps it had been better here when there was a king to impose some authority – perhaps an island needed that. Maybe the Mainland ways would not work here where life was so easy and without any threat of danger. Maybe . . .

She decided to seek out Chip. It was unlikely that his Bark-rush would have the answers, but Chip himself had a good brain and always seemed glad to talk with her.

At the Zwamp she found him crossly searching through the undergrowth.

"What are you looking for?" she asked.

"Someone's broken up my Bark-rush and thrown all the rings away," he said gruffly. "I've only found about seven. Can you help me look, please."

"Did a human do that?" she asked.

"No, it was squirrels, young ones. Their scent was all around here. Sycamore's and his hoppos I think. Sundamn him!"

"Chip," said Marguerite sternly. "You know I don't like that kind of language."

She helped him find the rest of the bark-rings and left him threading them on new rush-stems. She had found a number of sloe stones in the bushes and suspected that they had come from the leaf-pile where sloes were left each autumn by Caterpillar to ruddle in the heat. She went to the pile to see if there were any more there.

Lying next to the steaming leaves was Caterpillar himself, groaning and trying to rub his back with his paws.

Ruddled, she thought, ruddled old fool, and was about to pass him on the other side of the pile, when she remembered Dandelion's story and went over to him.

"Are you all right?" she asked.

"Uz've got thiz awful pain in uz back. Can yew vetch Voxglove or Cowzlip to zee me." He groaned again and a dribble of urine dropped onto a dead leaf. It was bright red.

"I'll get them at once," she told him and hurried off to the drey set aside for sick squirrels. Voxglove was there and Marguerite told her about Caterpillar.

"Painz in the back and blood in hiz piddle – that'z zervantz' zicknezz. Too many ruddled zloez!"

They hurried back together but were too late. Caterpillar was Sun-gone, but they were in time to drive away a magpie that was about to peck out his eyes.

While Voxglove went to fetch other squirrels to help bury the ex-zervant's body, Marguerite stayed near in case the magpie returned. Next to the leafpile was the blackthorn bush that was already laden with the dark green berries that would soon turn a dusky black as they ripened. She thought hard and could think of no other such bush on the island, though they were plentiful on the Mainland.

A daring idea came into her head. It was contrary to all that she had ever learned, especially the Kernel which old Burdock, her grandmother, had taught her.

> Squirrels protect trees,
> They have enough enemies,
> Treat them as your friends.

She looked round guiltily then, sure that she was not being observed, hopped over to the blackthorn and bit away a ring of bark all round the base. I may be killing a tree, she told herself, but I am saving many squirrels.

The exposed wood gleamed accusingly white so she rubbed soil into the raw wood until it was hardly noticeable, then brushed the dirt from her paws.

With the squirrels who had come to bury Caterpillar was Marguerite's daughter, Burdock the News-squirrel. She greeted her mother coolly then went and prodded Caterpillar's body. "How long has he been dead?" she asked.

Later when they were scratching leaves over his grave and saying the Farewell Kernel, Marguerite noticed Burdock looking closely at the base of the blackthorn bush.

The news was swiftly carried around the island.

DYING SQUIRREL KILLS THE TREE HE LOVED

Caterpillar, known for his fondness for ruddled
sloes, took a last final revenge on the tree that led
to his death . . .

In the concern over Caterpillar, Chip's annoyance at the
damage to his gadget seemed minor, but there was another
case of wilful damage reported the next day. All the little
Woodstocks, so lovingly trained around the hazel saplings
by Chestnut and Heather, were uprooted and left to die.
Sycamore was blamed and called before the council.

He sat there sullenly, his body radiating contempt.

"It has been reported," Clover the Tagger said, "that
you have wilfully destroyed trees despite knowing the
Kernel:

> *Squirrels protect treees,*
> *They have enough enemies,*
> *Treat them as your friends.*

"What have you to say for yourself?"

Marguerite felt very uncomfortable. Was what
Sycamore had allegedly done been so very different from
what she had done herself only the day before? At least she
had a motive. Perhaps Sycamore did too. Should she be
trying to find out? With no further thought she spoke out.

"I would like to suggest that this meeting is suspended
while Sycamore and I talk about his reasons in private. I
know it is against custom but please trust me. I am sure I
can help."

Clover said, "It *is* against custom, but so many things
that are happening now are against our customs. I value

Marguerite's judgement. Unless any squirrel is against, we will wait for Marguerite's report. Sycamore the Ruddled, you will do exactly what Marguerite tells you and answer all her questions. We meet again here in seven days." Marguerite signalled to Sycamore to follow her and the two left together.

"I want to know why you do all these things," she told him. "But don't answer now, I want you to think carefully before you tell me. I want the real reason, not whatever comes into your head – that's too easy. First though, we will go and apologise to Chip and see if he needs help remaking his Bark-rush."

Chip was not happy to see Marguerite with Sycamore. A tinge of jealousy stabbed him and he ignored the proffered apologies, turning away and scratching at a flea bite so vigorously that a trace of blood showed on his fur.

"Chip!" Marguerite said sternly. "Behave yourself. I look to you to set an example."

Chip looked contrite and mumbled his apology. Marguerite was staring at the blood on his fur, her mind obviously far away.

"Not bleeding – breeding!" she said out loud. "Woodlouse knows how the mushrooms of the moon control breeding. *That's* what Thizle was trying to tell me."

Then her face fell. Her dear friend Woodlouse (now called Wood Anemone), who appeared to hold the future of the Ourland squirrels in her paws, was out of reach. She had stayed on the Mainland to help with the teaching of the Greys.

Marguerite knew she must find a way to get a message to her.

Chapter 19

The stern-faced scoutmaster called his boy scouts together and instructed them to sit on the grass. He was not looking forward to what he had to say.

It was a pity. The camp had gone well so far. The boys had made bridges, rafts and bivouac shelters. They had all worked well together and played exciting wide-games and learned about stalking and concealment. Now this had happened to spoil it.

His knees were burning. Unaccustomed to short trousers, the last two sunny days had left their bright red mark. He wondered briefly if what he was going to have to announce was unfair but then decided crossly that the little blighters must be taught a lesson.

"I do feel that one or more of you have let the side down," he said. "This troop was selected from all the scouts in Dorset to camp here on Brownsea Island on the very place where Baden-Powell held the first ever scout camp nearly sixty years ago. That was a real privilege for our troop. Now someone has chopped a tree about so that it looks like a squirrel. I had to promise the wardens that all axe-work would be strictly supervised. I want the person who is responsible to own up."

He waited but no one spoke.

"Come on," he said. "Someone must have done it."

"Perhaps it was a squirrel done it," a young scout ventured.

The other scouts laughed nervously and the scoutmaster glowered.

"If no one owns up by lunch-time none of you will go to help launch the hot-air balloon this afternoon. Dismiss."

The scoutmaster went angrily back to his tent to rub calamine lotion on to his sunburnt knees. If none of the little blighters owned up he would have to miss seeing the flight himself.

Away from his hoppos, and with no access to the ruddled sloes, Sycamore was really pleasant company. After his apology to Chip he seemed eager to learn numbers from Marguerite and find out what the Bark-rush could be used for. She told him of her concern about the possibility of the island becoming overpopulated by squirrels and she reminded him of the dreadful plague that had virtually wiped out the rabbits earlier in the year. Then Chip, at first reluctantly, taught him how to calculate using the bark rings. Marguerite sat apart from them, trying to think of a way to get a message to Wood Anemone.

Later on that hot afternoon, the three of them were together, resting in one of the trees that formed the Island Screen. Chip seemed unhappy that Marguerite planned to spend so much time alone with Sycamore and when she had suggested they go to look at the Mainland from the South Shore trees, he had tagged along.

"What in the Sunless Pit is *that*?" Sycamore asked, when

135

a roar as of some great animal came from the direction of the meadow between them and the church.

Moments later the sound came again and the three squirrels hurried through the trees to where they could look out over the open grassy area. They could see a few humans gathered round a hump, the colour of a buttercup flower, which billowed and rippled in the breeze. Nearby a peacock and his harem of peahens scratched and pecked at the ground as though nothing unusual was happening.

"What's that thing?" Sycamore asked again in a hushed voice.

"I don't know, I've seen nothing like it before," Marguerite replied, climbing higher for a better view.

There was a longer roar and the glossy yellow hump, seeming to have a life of its own, rose above the heads of the humans and tossed about in the breeze. An unfamiliar and disturbing burning smell blew directly towards the squirrels in the pine. The humans were now clustered below the yellow thing, which had become a round ball, and were holding something beneath it that the squirrels could not see.

"It's the Suns-child," whispered Marguerite, "come again!"

"What's the Suns-child?" Sycamore asked, hoping for a better answer this time.

"Twice in the past, the Sun has sent its child when we squirrels have been in trouble. Now it's here again, only it's grown much bigger. Look at the size of it!"

The balloon towered above the humans who were debating amongst themselves as to whether or not it was safe to fly with the wind rising and blowing so strongly from east to west. The pilot was annoyed that the boy scouts had not turned up as promised to help with holding the basket, even though a boy had come at the last minute with an apologetic message.

Finally, having decided that it was *not* safe, the pilot tried to release the hot air but the ripcord seemed to have jammed. With the other helpers hanging grimly on to the basket, he climbed onto the woven wicker edge and reached upwards for the cord.

He was doing this when a sudden swirl of wind spun across the meadow, lifting the dried soil from the peacocks' dusting places, and blowing it into the eyes of those around the balloon. Each, believing that others were holding it down, let go to wipe their eyes. The balloon suddenly lifted. The pilot, also temporarily blinded, let go and fell backwards off the basket, knocking two of the helpers to the ground.

The balloon jerked violently away, rose higher and floated off in a westerly direction towards the trees, trailing a rope.

"Grab that rope someone. Grab hold of that rope," the pilot shouted, getting to his feet and running after the balloon which was now nearly above the trees. Others joined the chase.

The squirrels heard the incomprehensible shouting and saw the humans running after the tail-end of the rope, now far out of their reach. It trailed through the branches towards them.

Marguerite sensed that the Suns-child should be restrained and called to Chip and Sycamore, "Help me catch that rope, we must help the Suns-child," and snatched at the trailing line as it slithered past them.

In a moment, the three squirrels, all clutching the rope, had been torn from the treetop and were being lifted bodily high into the air. "Hang on for your lives," Marguerite shouted.

It was suddenly calm and, looking down, Marguerite could see the island falling away behind them. Below was the blue water of Poole Harbour, dotted with the white spots of boat sails. There was no sensation of dizziness as there had been when she had once climbed the chalk cliff to the Barrow of the Flowers. Somehow the ground was remote and distant, not a part of the world they now found themselves in.

"Climb up after me," she called down to Chip and Sycamore and the three climbed easily, their claws gripping firmly into the fibres of the rope until they reached the basket and scrambled over the padded edge. They explored the box of woven willow stems, which contained only a few loose items of human's coverings and two round red metal things as big as tree stumps.

Marguerite was puzzled by the silence. Apart from the occasional creaking of the willow box, there was no sound at all. Down in the trees the wind had been singing its gentle song, so familiar to the squirrels that they hardly noticed it. There pine needles had rubbed against one another, leaves shook and rustled and the movement of air past the twigs and branches always had a special sound of its own.

Suddenly she realised what had made the change – they were floating and drifting on the very wind itself!

How many times had she watched the white-winged gulls flying effortlessly on the breezes over the sea and envied them? Now she and her companions were doing the same. Her tail rose with pleasure as they climbed to the edge of the basket and sat there, claws gripping the soft padding.

"We are flying on the wind," she shouted and Sycamore grinned across at Chip. This was *much* more fun than the stupid things he had been doing lately.

There was land below them now and the Suns-child seemed to be slowly getting nearer the ground as they drifted along.

"There's the Blue Pool," Marguerite said excitedly, as she recognised her old home demesne, the pool itself glowing sapphire in the green trees, below and to the south of them. The Sun had sent its child once again to help her and now it was carrying her to Wood Anemone. She prepared herself for the Suns-child to come down out of the sky but it floated on.

Perplexed, Marguerite recited the Kernel:

> *Trust in the Sun.*
> *His ways are mysterious.*
> *Faith can fell fir trees.*

"That must be Rowans's Pool down there." She pointed out another small pool now passing beneath them, shaped like a crouching animal with an island where its eye would have been. And still the Suns-child floated on.

> *Have faith in the Sun*
> *His ways are mysterious . . .*

Rowan looked up and saw the yellow balloon above the three trees of his Eyeland.

"The Suns-child has come again to save us," he called, and the besieged squirrels followed his pointing claw, then saw his face fall as the great yellow ball, its fabric now billowing lazily in the wind, drifted westwards apparently without seeing them.

The balloon floated on, the wind veering slightly and blowing more from the north-east. Below them, Marguerite could hear the gun-fire from the Lulworth ranges and see the flashes as the humans played with the thunder and lightning force. The Suns-child was now much nearer the ground and heading for a ridge of hills, beyond which she caught glimpses of the sea.

As it dropped even more the basket bumped along the ground on the top of the ridge, and their movement slowed briefly. Before the squirrels, tumbled in the bottom of the basket, could compose themselves and jump clear, it lifted again and floated feebly out towards the sea. Then, as if giving up, the Suns-child collapsed with its flaccid skin draping the mellow stone walls of a ruined barn.

"That was fun," said Sycamore, crawling from the basket and brushing himself down, followed by Marguerite and Chip who did the same. "Where do we go from here?"

The sun was setting, painting the sky in dramatic shades of gold and red, all reflected in the waters of the circular cove to their right. A great mass of rock far out to sea in the south-west was dark against the glow. Chip pointed to it. "That's the Isle of Portland. That's where I was born," he told Sycamore.

Rowan had watched the Suns-child disappear and suddenly felt very tired. He looked at the bright western sky and the setting sun.

> *In times of great stress*
> *Rest is a sound investment –*
> *Restoring one's strength.*

"Organise the night watch again, Spindle-Friend," he said, "but count me in this night."

He went into the ground-drey, curled up and closed his eyes.

On Ourland, a Council Meeting had been called and was better attended than most.

Just Poplar called for order.

"Doez any zquirrel know what huz happened to Marguerite, Chip and Zycamore? They zeem to have left Ourland with the round yellow thing the humanz brought here. The thing that looked like the Zun and floated in the zky?"

Chapter 20

The humans arrived at the ruined barn as it was getting dark, folded the Suns-child and carried it, with its basket, away into the night. The three squirrels hid in holes in the decaying stonework until the humans had gone, then climbed up to the highest point and looked around.

Somehow we've got to get back to the Blue Pool, Marguerite was thinking. But if the Sun had meant us to go there, why has the Suns-child brought us to the coast?

She turned towards Portland far across the bay and watched as it seemed to sink into the water as the light faded from the sky. Stars appeared, twinkling and sparkling above her head and she sensed a sadness trapped in the stone walls below her. Chip seemed to feel it too and he urged her to leave.

"Wait," she said. "Hush." She had felt tingling at the base of her whiskers which usually indicated that the dolphins were trying to contact her. She cleared her mind to listen.

It was Lundy's lone voice she heard, and by turning her head, she could locate its direction – far out in the sea to the south.

There was an urgency and concern in it that was new to her. Marguerite had only ever known calmness in the dolphins' voices – except when Malin spoke about pollution. Lundy's voice was far from calm now.

"Squirrel-friend, where are you? I am on my way to your island to find you, but I sense that you are not there, but are somewhere nearer."

Marguerite projected her thoughts seaward. "I am here with two friends. We are near a place where the sea is in a circle with land almost all round it. Do you know this place?"

"That must be the Cove of Lulworth. I'll come at once. Can you get down to the water's edge? I need your help – desperately!"

Marguerite roused her companions, who were dozing near her, and in the light of a moon that was now casting a silver sheen over the seascape, she told them what she had just heard.

"The dolphins need us. Lundy is coming to meet us soon. We must go down to the edge of the water in that round hollow."

Treading warily and alert for night-danger they went along a stony Man-track and through a wire fence, then under dark bushes the foliage of which was permanently bent landwards by winds from the sea. Slippery paths and steps took them down to the shore.

The water in the bay was calm and lapped quietly on the shingle beach. Smells of damp and rotting seaweed filled their noses as they waited, looking towards the gap in the cliffs with the open sea beyond. Soon a black shape, a dorsal fin clearly visible in the moonlight, rose from the water some distance from the shore, and they heard the sound of air being blown through the nostril on top of a dolphin's head.

"We are here, Lundy-Friend," Marguerite called.

"I am pleased that you were so near. My prayer must have been heard."

"The Suns-child brought us," Marguerite replied. "You prayed for us to come?"

"It's Finisterre. He's tangled in a human's fish-net on the other side of the Bank of Chesils. He is safe at the moment lying on the pebbles, but there is a storm coming and the net is stopping him from swimming."

Marguerite looked up at the night sky and remembered the sunset.

A red sky at night
Heralds a delightful day –
Dawn to dusk sunshine.

"Are you sure about a storm?" she asked.

"Yes, the red sky was deceiving. The wind is shifting to the west and then the south-west and a storm is coming. We have learned a lot about the weather in the last * ⸎ ⸎ ⸎ years. Believe me!"

"I do," said Marguerite. "How can we help?" Wood Anemone and the troubles on Ourland were forgotten.

"I must find a way to get you to Finisterre before the storm reaches him. Can your teeth cut away the Man-cords of the net."

* ⸎ ⸎ ⸎ = 60 x 60 x 60 = 216,000 years.

"We will do all we can," Marguerite replied, "Can you get a boat?"

"There won't be time for that – can you hold on to some wood if I carry it in my mouth?"

"We will do our best. Have you brought some wood?"

"No, can you find some on the shore? Please hurry."

Marguerite quickly explained the situation to Sycamore who had only heard one side of the conversation and the three squirrels scurried along the high-tide mark, searching for a suitable piece of driftwood. Lundy, in the water, kept pace with them, her agitation sweeping in waves towards the land.

At first there was a total absence of wood, the glowing embers of a human's fire explaining this. They briefly watched the tiny flames, some blue from the salt in the wood and others a soft green around a copper nail. Marguerite hustled them on until, farther along, Sycamore found the handle of a broken oar, half-buried in the slimy ribbons of kelpweed. They struggled to free it, tiny crabs scuttling for cover as they did so, then rolled it down the beach to the water's edge.

"What now?" Marguerite called out to Lundy.

"Are you *all* coming?"

Marguerite looked at the others.

"Yes," said Chip simply, and once Sycamore had been told he said, "Wouldn't miss this for all the nuts on Ourland."

The squirrels grasped the wood, Chip and Marguerite at one end, Sycamore at the other.

"Hold tightly to the wood – I'm coming in."

There was a rush of water as the dolphin surged towards

the beach and the squirrels felt the oar handle being picked up and held high, as the great black body thrashed in the shallows and turned about. Then, with another heave and a violent beating of her tail, Lundy was in deep water again, holding the oar handle crossways in her mouth. All three squirrels were soaked and, as the dolphin swam rapidly towards the opening from the bay into the open sea, a cold night wind blowing from the south-west quickly chilled them.

Lundy was right about the wind changing, thought Marguerite, digging her claws deeper through the layers of peeling varnish and into the soft wood below.

"Thank you all. Hold on tightly." Lundy let her thoughts envelop the squirrels, then she closed her mind to interrogation and tuned in to the minds of each squirrel in turn.

The young one is enjoying this; it's nothing more than a great adventure to him. The other male is here because Marguerite is here, he would follow her anywhere. He loves her – I wonder if she knows?

Marguerite, my friend, I seem to know you so well. You have never even thought of Chip as a suitor. You really *do* want to help me and you have such complete trust in your Sun that you *now* believe you have been sent to do that. This is a strange friendship – but one I value highly.

Lundy reopened her mind as she swam steadily on; Marguerite was asking how far they had to go.

"I came round the end of the Isle of Portland, through the tearing waters of the Race, but we won't go back that way. We are swimming the Bay of Weymouth and then we'll cross the Harbour of Portland to the Lagoon of Fleet, between the Bank of Chesils and the Mainland. Malin and Finisterre are on the seaward side of the pebble bank, with other dolphins helping, but none have teeth to cut like yours can. We should be there soon after dawn – if my strength holds."

Marguerite sensed that swimming with her head out of water was tiring Lundy. She would normally swim submerged, only coming up to breathe.

Occasionally the dolphin changed course slightly to take advantage of the different currents that she seemed to know intimately. She was holding the oar-handle steady and firm, and by the time they passed between the great rocks forming the breakwater that protected the ships in the Harbour of Portland, the squirrels' fur had dried in the wind.

"The tide is against us," Lundy told Marguerite, and the squirrel sensed the extra energy the dolphin was having to expend to swim against the mass of water rushing out through the narrow gap.

The moon was turning pale and the dawn showed grey behind them. Huge metal cylinders leaned with the flow, the seaweed and barnacles on the undersides and the anchor chains of the giant buoys smelling dank and salty on the morning air. Lundy swam doggedly on against the current.

At the Ferry-bridge they passed under the metal girders, past the round black bridge supports where the whole weight of water trapped in the lagoon was trying to follow the moon's pull and rush out into the Harbour before the earth rotated enough for it to be drawn back to fill the lagoon once again.

Marguerite knew that Lundy's strength was failing. "You must rest," she told her.

> *In times of great stress*
> *Rest is a sound investment –*
> *Restoring one's strength.*

"I can't," she replied. "The storm is too close. My son will be battered to death on the beach."

Unexpectedly Chip who, with Sycamore had been concentrating on holding tight to the oar-handle said,

> *When quite exhausted*
> *Keep on going while you must,*
> *Never, ever quit.*

"I won't," Lundy responded, and Marguerite asked Chip where he had learned this Kernel. She was sure that she had not heard it before.

"I don't know," he told her, "it just came into my head. They often do."

Marguerite turned her attention back to Lundy. "Can you make it?" she asked.

"I will. We dolphins have a saying—"

> *If you think you can,*
> *Or if you think you cannot*
> *Either way it's true.*
> *Sun and Sea will support you –*
> *Buoy your determination.*

Lundy swam doggedly on.

"We have a saying like that too," Marguerite said and then was silent, to let the dolphin concentrate on her swimming.

They had passed the boatworks and the caravan park on their right side and a gaggle of fishermen's huts on the pebbles to their left, and Lundy was now forcing herself to swim against the tidal flow at the narrows where the buildings of the Army Bridging Camp loomed against the sky.

The black heads of cormorants bobbed up around them then disappeared as the birds dived, only to reappear with small flatfish in their beaks which they swallowed awkwardly, their thoats bulging as the fish went down. Others, fully gorged, sat on the concrete ramp their wings spread to catch a drying wind.

The flow eased as the lagoon widened but Marguerite could sense Lundy's strength ebbing. "Come on, my friend – If you think you can . . . I know you can, I know you can. Carry us to your Finisterre."

She felt the exhausted dolphin find new reserves and surge forward again. "You can, you can, YOU CAN," Marguerite urged her as more dolphin voices within her head were joining her own.

"Lundy," one was saying. "Keep going, we are here with Finisterre. Keep going. You have the squirrel with you?"

"Better than that," Lundy responded, her tiredness apparent in every wave of her voice. "I have *three* squirrels."

"Keep going. Bring them to us. Keep going. Lundy, keep swimming."

Chapter 21

As dawn broke, the dolphin swam into shallow water on the Chesil Bank side of the Fleet Lagoon. On the pebbled shore were several large white birds. The squirrels recognised them as swans, even though they had never been near any of them whenever they had flown in and landed on the lagoon at Ourland.

Lundy's head drooped and the oar-handle floated out of her mouth, rolling over in the water with the weight of the squirrels.

Marguerite let go of the wood and called to the others, "Swim to the beach."

Chip and Sycamore followed her through the brackish water and crawled onto the pebbles. Cold and bedraggled, they shook themselves and blinked the water from their eyes, only to find a pair of swans, their necks bent low, hissing fiercely at them. Before this hostile reception they had no choice but to retreat back into the cold water.

"LEAVE – THESE CREATURES – ALONE."

It was Lundy's voice, speaking slowly and with great authority. The swans raised their necks, waved their heads from side to side and walked away as though the squirrels no longer existed.

"Please, my friends, go over the bank to help my son. I must rest here. Come back to me when you are successful. Go now, please!" Lundy pleaded.

Wet from their swim ashore, tired from lack of sleep and stiff from many hours clinging to the oar, the three squirrels scrambled over the shingles to the top of the bank.

Though the sky was clear, the wind, now blowing strongly from the south-west, was forcing huge waves to roll in from the bay and crash onto the shingle. The wind tore and tugged at their ears and tails and buffeted their chill damp bodies. On the beach, being thrown about by the waves, they could see the young dolphin, its flippers entangled in a mass of fine white threads. Just seaward of it, a semi-circle of dolphins who were trying to shelter it were themselves frequently getting tossed up onto the beach. They would then roll back with the undertow and swim out to try and stem the force of waves once more.

Marguerite stood on her hind-legs to assess the situation before acting. The dolphins, seeing her tiny body silhouetted against the skyline, sent waves of welcome through the air to envelop her and her companions. She recognised Malin's voice as he greeted her.

"What should we do?" She focused her thoughts on him.

"Can you reach Finisterre and bite away the net?" There was a desperate pleading in his thought-voice. "Are your teeth strong enough?"

"We will try," Marguerite replied aloud. "If you think you can . . ."

Her voice was lost in the roar of an even bigger wave

rushing up the beach towards her. She turned to Chip and Sycamore.

"Follow me," she said, and scurried down the pebbles.

The three reached the water's edge just as a wave was withdrawing. They followed the retreating line of foam as far as the young dolphin who was eyeing them thankfully.

Each squirrel grabbed at the tangle of fine nylon threads, and held on tightly, biting vigorously until the next wave came crashing in and smothered them in salt water and sea-foam. They hung on, holding their breaths as the wave spent its energy and rolled back, then started biting again, severing the thin hard filaments one by one. Blood seeped through the tangled mass where these had cut into the dolphin's smooth black skin.

"I'll go to the other side," Sycamore shouted above the roar as yet another wave rushed in to submerge them. As he clambered over Finisterre's slippery back, the wave tore him free and the undertow dragged him down the wet pebbles and sucked his squirming body into deep water. The next wave towered up.

I'm going to drown, he thought as his lungs filled with salt water and he struggled frantically towards the surface. Then he felt himself caught in a gentle mouth and he was lifted clear of the wave while he coughed and coughed and coughed.

A voice enveloped him, "Can you carry on, or do you need to rest?"

"Carry on," he responded and Malin surfed in on the next wave to deposit Sycamore once again on Finisterre's left side. On the stranded dolphin's other side, Marguerite and Chip were still biting and gnawing, their teeth and jaws aching with their efforts. Malin lay on the shingle at Finisterre's tail ready to catch at any squirrel who might lose its grip, his huge bulk helping to break the rush of each wave.

The tangle of nylon was beginning to come free and more blood was flowing from the dolphin's wounds as they tugged and pulled at the severed filaments. Suddenly the whole mass came loose and was drawn down the beach by a retreating wave, the three squirrels rolling with it as they clung on.

Malin caught the ball of nylon filaments in his mouth and surged up the beach on the next wave to drop it just above the highest point reached by the waves. He turned and pushed Finisterre into deeper water as other dolphins swam forward to help support the youngster with their bodies.

The next wave to reach the squirrels was a chorus of "Thank you" from the dolphins in the sea. The squirrels dragged their tired and aching bodies a little further up the beach.

As they lay there, Marguerite picked up instructions being given by Lundy on the other side of the bank.

"THREE SWANS —

GO TO THE FAR SIDE OF THE RIDGE —

FIND THE THREE SMALL ANIMALS —

PICK THEM UP — CAREFULLY —

BRING THEM TO THE SHORE HERE —

AWAIT INSTRUCTIONS —

ACTION NOW —"

A few minutes later three white heads with orange beaks and black masks, appeared on the skyline.

Chip did not see them. Tired as he was, something else had attracted his attention. Immediately under his right paw was one of the bright yellow discs of soft metal that he had once found near the Portland end of the beach and which his father had discarded as useless. It gleamed in the sunshine and he turned it over. There was a Man-head on the one side and indecipherable squiggles on the other. He wanted to keep it more than anything he had ever wanted before. As he drew it to his body, he felt the skin on the back of his neck gripped firmly and he was lifted into the air, still clutching the golden disc.

Dangling there wriggling helplessly, he saw that Marguerite and Sycamore were being treated in the same way and the three swans carried the squirrels over the beach and down to the shore on the sheltered side. The storm-clouds, that had been massing on the horizon, covered the sun and cold rain came driving in towards the land.

"SWANS —

THESE ANIMALS ARE AS PRECIOUS AS UNHATCHED EGGS —

ONE SWAN — SHELTER THEM —

TWO SWANS — FETCH GRAIN-FOOD FROM THE MEN ACROSS THE WATER OF THE FLEET —

ACTION NOW —"

Lundy was still lying in the shallow water issuing instructions to the swans, who reacted to her programming exactly. One scratched a hollow in the tide-wrack and each lowered their squirrel into it as the rain came slashing down the beach. One swan spread its wings and settled over the three weak animals, warming them with the heat of its body. The other two swans waded into the water and swam through the storm towards the Mainland.

After the initial feeling of being smothered, the squirrels found that they could breathe easily, air moving freely through the feathers. Underneath the swan it was dry and snug, and as they sheltered their fur dried and their teeth stopped chattering. One by one they fell asleep.

The storm had passed when Marguerite awoke and peered out at the clean-washed world from under the swan's wing. There was a small pile of wheat-grains near her and she woke Chip and Sycamore to share a meal. The swan seemed content to stay where she was.

In the evening sunlight Marguerite could see Lundy's fin sticking up out of the water and projected her thoughts in that direction.

"Lundy-Friend, are you all right?"

The fin moved and Lundy's head appeared above the water; Marguerite could just see her usual grin.

"Yes, I'm stronger now. I've never been so tired. Malin tells me you saved Finisterre. We can never thank you enough."

"Is Finisterre safe? I was concerned about his injuries."

"We believe so. He is young and fit and the sea water helps the healing if it is not polluted. It is clean here at present. He should be himself again soon."

"What will you do now?" Marguerite asked.

"I am resting here tonight. You must do the same. Stay under the swan; you will be safe and warm there. Then we must find the best way to take you back to your island. After that I will rejoin Malin and Finisterre."

"Will that be difficult?"

"Oh, no. Think how easily I can contact you when I put my mind to it. What is your friend holding?"

Marguerite saw that Chip was hugging a disc of bright metal. She described it to Lundy.

"A golden coin. We know where there are many of those on the seabed. Humans rate them highly. They are pretty but not worth fighting over."

"Humans fight for those?"

"Fight *and* kill one another."

Marguerite took another look at the coin.

People puzzle us
With their strange actions – but then
They're only Human.

When the moon rose that night, a hungry fox padded along the walk-way through the rushes and onto the pebbles of the beach. He had found no Man-scraps and had failed to catch even a mouse. He scented the air, no food-smell there, so he followed the shore of the Fleet Lagoon hoping to find a dead bird or a fish on the tide-line.

He passed the Dragon's Teeth. To the fox these huge weathered concrete blocks had always been there; seemingly as old as the medieval chapel on the hill opposite.

The fox saw the three sleeping swans and walked towards them cautiously, puzzled by an apparent scent of squirrel mixed with the familiar swan-scent. He did not approach too closely – all local foxes had tried to tackle a swan once, but only once. He turned up the beach to follow a faint blood-smell that was teasing his nostrils.

On the pebbles over the ridge he found the ball of nylon that had nearly caused the death of Finisterre and had now been blown up the bank by the force of the gale. He crept towards it, nose twitching. The blood he could smell was inside it. He licked the nylon, then tried to push his nose further into the tangled mass. A thread caught behind a tooth; the other side of the loop under his lower jaw. He tried to push the loop off and his right paw caught in another. His left paw could not free it either, and then that too was tangled. Soon a back paw was also trapped and, growling and struggling, the fox rolled down towards the breaking waves which were rushing up the beach as if they had a hunger greater even than his own.

His one free paw reached forward in a last effort to disentangle himself and as it did so a Seventh Wave towered higher than the rest, crashed onto the pebbles, roared up towards the helpless fox and dragged him down into the deep water off-shore.

That night the scavenging conger eels learned a new taste, though by dawn one of their number was himself trapped by the fine filaments. Later, crabs dined on the body of that conger eel. When the net was finally thrown up the beach again, a human burned it in a pile of driftwood, along with the empty carapaces of a dozen crabs and, the body of a herring gull that had been tempted by the crab meat.

Unaware of the drama being played out so close to her, Marguerite, warm under the swan, dreamed of their flight in the balloon. A new and exciting idea was filling her head when she woke.

Chapter 22

"Lundy, are you awake?"

Marguerite projected her thought towards the black fin, visible in the dawn-still waters of the Fleet. The rumble of the waves on the far side of the Chesil Bank could just be heard, but the wind had died away during the night.

"I am here, we don't sleep in the same way as land animals."

"How do you get the swans to do what you want them to do?" Marguerite asked.

"Birds have simple brains. Mostly they act as their instincts direct and do not reason as we do. If you can reach their brains with clear instructions they follow those instead of their instincts. You heard me do it yesterday."

"Is that a right thing to do; to dominate another creature for your own benefit?" Marguerite asked.

"Not if it will harm that creature and the need is trifling. What I did yesterday saved you from cold-death and did not harm the swans. They are only passing time now until their next nesting season."

"Could *I* dominate them?" Marguerite asked.

"*If you think you can* . . . Try repeating what I say, slowly and positively. I will submerge my thoughts so that it is yours that reach them. Swans – "

"SWANS –" repeated Marguerite and the three swans nearby raised their heads.

"Fetch me a pebble – Action now – "

"FETCH ME A PEBBLE –

ACTION NOW – "

Each swan picked up a pebble, brought it to Marguerite, laid it at her feet and stepped back to wait for more instructions.

Chip and Sycamore, who had only heard part of the "conversation", watched in amazement, Chip still clutching the golden coin.

"Do you think the swans would carry us through the air, flying to Ourland or the Blue Pool?" Marguerite asked.

"For an Innocent, you do have imaginative ideas," Lundy replied.

Marguerite knew that "Innocent" was the dolphin word for smaller-brained animals, and was not offended as she knew that literally it must be true.

"Each swan could easily carry one of you," Lundy went on. "But it's probably never been done before. Would you risk it?"

"At one time, *everything* we do had never been done before," said Marguerite, thinking of all the stories of Acorn, the first squirrel in the world. "But I think I will practise instructing the swans first.

THREE SWANS –

SWIM ACROSS THE FLEET –

SWIM BACK TO ME –

ACTION NOW – "

Within an hour, Marguerite was confident of success and was briefing her companions on her plans.

"We will each climb onto a swan's back and grip the feathers tightly. Hold as many feathers as you can with each paw but do not hurt the swans. I will give them instructions to take us to the Blue Pool where I have to talk to Wood Anemone. Then we will fly on to Ourland. After that I will give the swans directions to return. Chip, I think you will have to leave your metal disk here."

Chip looked crestfallen. "I *would* like to take it. I think I could hold it under my body. If it slips out and falls I don't have it any more – but then I don't if I leave it here."

"Very well," Marguerite told him, sensing how important it must be to him. "But don't risk falling yourself trying to catch it. It's not like falling from a tree – we've all done that. We will be a lot higher – like we were in the Sunschild."

Lundy had her head out of the water, watching with great interest as Marguerite instructed the swans.

"THREE SWANS –

SOON YOU WILL EACH PICK UP ONE OF US SQUIRRELS –

YOU WILL PLACE YOUR SQUIRREL ON YOUR BACK AND WAIT WHILE IT TAKES A FIRM HOLD – IT WILL NOT HURT YOU –

YOU WILL WADE INTO DEEP WATER AND THEN YOU WILL FLY EASTWARDS ABOVE THE BEACH TO THE BRIDGE –

FROM THERE YOU WILL FLY ACROSS THE SEA TO THE COVE OF LULWORTH

WHERE THE SEA IS HELD IN A RING OF CLIFFS –

FROM THERE YOU WILL FLY US TO A POOL WHERE
THE WATER IS BRIGHT BLUE –

Do you know this place?"

The three heads bowed "Yes".

"YOU WILL LAND ON THE WATER THERE –
YOU WILL TAKE US TO THE SHORE –
YOU WILL THEN RECEIVE MORE INSTRUCTIONS –

By tonight you will be back here. Thank you for your
cooperation.

ACTION NOW – "

Lundy watched the swans pick up a squirrel each, as
they had done the day before, lift it round onto their backs
and, shortly afterwards wade out into the calm water.

Marguerite's farewells blended with her own as, one
behind the other, the swans ran across the water, their feet
making less and less commotion as the great white wings
swept the air away below them. Then there was no sound
but the W-wow, W-wow, of the wing-beats. Two of the
swans dropped back slightly to take advantage of the easier
flying in the turbulence created by the leader's flight, and
the V formation climbed higher and disappeared into the
distance.

Lundy swam leisurely down the lagoon towards
Portland Harbour, the open sea and reunion with her
family.

Chapter 23

The wings of the three swans beat steadily. The formation had reached the height chosen by the leader and they flew above the beach until they passed over the Ferry-bridge, then turned slightly to fly across Portland Harbour.

At first Marguerite had clung tightly to the swan's back, her head buried in the feathers. As she gained confidence, she lifted her head and, moving one paw-hold at a time, edged forward until she could look down past the side of the bird's neck. Far below she could see the curve of the pebble beach reaching out to the great rock of Portland, the waves seeming to wriggle along the shore like a grass snake swimming after frogs. How different it all looked from up here compared with the roaring and crashing they had suffered the day before.

The wings beat rhythmically, W-wow, W-wow, W-wow.

Below her the humans' travelling boxes were crossing the bridge and then the swans were over the grey ships at anchor in the harbour. Flying seemed so effortless compared with the strain Lundy had suffered carrying them the day before.

Was that really only the day before?

She recognised the harbour breakwaters and, raising her head, she could see the white cliffs on the far side of Weymouth Bay. The great wings rose and fell, rose and fell, the air hissing through the pinion feathers, W-wow, W-wow, W-wow.

She turned to look at Chip and Sycamore. They grinned at her past their swans' heads.

With the distinctive shape of Lulworth Cove below them, she felt the change of direction that would take them across the land to the Blue Pool. Her instructions were being followed exactly and it would not be long before she was with Wood Anemone, learning the secret of the mushrooms of the moon. It would be good to see her friend again.

Rowan and Bluebell were aiming the Woodstock at the top of the bank across the pool from the Eyeland. Bluebell had caught a glimpse of grey fur and had pointed out the position to her father. He had calculated that a $\mathbf{6}$ would be required to curl whiskers and incapacitate any Grey at that distance. He rehearsed the movement and stood alert, the Woodstock sighted on the top of the bank, Bluebell standing behind him.

"Now," she shouted as a grey head showed, and Rowan scratched a $\mathbf{6}$ on the bare wood. The head dropped back behind the bank at the very moment that the shape of three flying swans appeared over the horizon in the same direction.

The invisible, spiralling force, though weak at that extreme range, seriously affected the birds. Their wing beats faltered, they lost formation and, fluttering and flapping out of control, they tumbled through the air then, seeming to recover somewhat, spread their wings and turned to make a long glide towards the open water of the pool.

Marguerite was enjoying the flight when the Woodstock's power-wave stuck. Reacting as quickly as she would when a gust of wind struck a branch on which she was sitting, she grasped the feathers tightly and hung on as the swans fell out of the sky. She fought to dominate their thoughts.

"SWANS —

FLY —

FLY —

ACTION NOW —

FLY —

ACTION NOW —

SPREAD YOUR WINGS —

HOLD THEM FIRM —

MAKE FOR THAT WATER BELOW —

ACTION NOW —

ACTION NOW —

LAND ON THE WATER —

ACTION NOW — "

The swans lowered their webbed feet, twisted their wings to resist the air and slid across the surface of the pool, then stopped, shaking their heads and hissing angrily.

"SWANS —

YOU ARE SAFE NOW —

RELAX —

ACTION NOW — "

In the silence that followed, the swans paddled gently

along the pool, dipping their heads under the water as if to clear their brains, then lifting them and shaking off droplets of water.

"What happened?" Chip called across to Marguerite. "My whiskers are hurting."

"So are mine," she said. "I feel like someone has used a Woodstock on me."

"Marguerite, Marguerite."

Marguerite was sure that she could hear her brother's voice calling her – but it was just not possible. Whatever force had brought the swans down out of the sky had clearly addled her brain.

"Marguerite. We're here. Here on the Eyeland."

"SWANS –

TAKE US TO THE ISLAND –

THAT WAY –

ACTION NOW – "

The great white birds, each with a squirrel sitting upright on its back, paddled along the pool, past the pink and white water lilies and waddled ashore onto the island near the pool's end. As they did so, Chip, clutching the golden coin, lost his balance and the coin fell into the orangy-brown water near the Eyeland shore.

"Marguerite!"

"Rowan! Meadowsweet! Bluebell!"

Marguerite had an overwhelming feeling that this had all happened before, then realised that it had, in that summer when they had journeyed from the coast to win back the Blue Pool Demesne from the Silver Tide.

Now though, she also recognised the feeling of being in a battle-zone. She brushed whiskers briefly with her brother and his life-mate and her handsome young niece, saw the Woodstock on the ground at Rowan's side then said, "What's going on here?"

"We are surrounded by Greys, led by one of the Three Lords. There has been a change of leader at Woburn and we were trying to escape to join you on Ourland. Were you really *flying* on these swans?"

"Yes. I'll explain later. How many Greys are there?"

"Lots," said Rowan, and Marguerite regretted never having found the time to teach her brother to count above eight.

"Lots, or Lots and Lots?"

"Lots and Lots!" Rowan replied and Marguerite noted the tiredness in his voice.

He led her up the mound to the top of the Eyeland, Bluebell and Meadowsweet dragging the Woodstock between them. A tree trunk lay across the water from the Mainland, forming a bridge. It had not been there when she had last seen the Eyeland.

Clustered near the bridge were the two ex-zervantz and their daughters, all looking bright-eyed if rather tired and thin.

Most surprising of all, there was a Grey on that side of the bridge, amongst the Reds.

"Wood Anemone-Friend, Spindle-Friend," she called and they turned to look up at her.

"Marguerite-Ma'am," said Wood Anemone.

"Marguerite-Friend, please."

"Marguerite-Friend. Where have you come from? Did you drop out of the sky?"

"Something like that. Look out behind you!" she shouted.

A phalanx of grey bodies was moving purposefully down towards the far end of the bridge.

"Heads down," shouted Meadowsweet to the squirrels below, and as they turned their backs on her, she swung the Woodstock towards the Greys and scratched a 3 on the bare wood.

Some of the attackers turned and scrambled back up and over the bank while others rolled down onto the level ground at the far end of the bridge, pawing at their whiskers, before wriggling back up the slope and out of sight. The Reds watched them go.

Rowan said, "We get a charge like that several times a day – they're not giving up easily. I don't know where they're all coming from. The trouble is we don't know how much power is left in the Woodstock – there can't be much now."

Marguerite glanced at the Grey, it seemed foolish to be giving away their weakness in front of one of the enemy.

Rowan saw her look. "Don't worry about Hickory, he's a Sun-squirrel. He's with us."

Marguerite looked across the water. There were no Greys in sight now and she went down to the bridge-end with Chip and Sycamore to make the formal introductions and greetings. She brushed whiskers with them all, even Hickory. Though she remembered him as one of the enemy leaders at the Battle of the Agglestone, he was obviously trusted and respected here.

Chapter 24

Rowan's and Marguerite's groups exchanged news while watching the banks for signs of another attack. Chip was at the water's edge peering down at the place where they had come ashore but was unable to see anything as the swans' feet had stirred up the clay making the water a milky white. The swans themselves were now feeding quietly in the water, reaching down with their long necks and searching the pool bottom for tasty morsels.

Marguerite's mind was already formulating an escape plan. She stood up and looked along the pool.

"SWANS —"

The swans raised their heads.

"CAN YOU FLY WITH TWO SQUIRRELS EACH?"

The swans raised their heads in unison.

"CAN YOU FLY WITH THREE SQUIRRELS EACH?"

The swans appeared to consult each other, then shook their heads violently.

"THANK YOU — STAY CLOSE."

She counted their combined party and did some calculations, wishing that she had Chip's Bark-rush to help. She called Chip over and explained the problem. He counted on his claws.

"With three swans, six squirrels can go at a time, so if six go on the first flight and one squirrel comes back, we then have five, and with the one who came back, that'll make up six for the second flight – two for each swan. No problem."

It was decided that Marguerite was to take the other five females on the first flight and return for the five males on the second.

Lord Malachite had seen the swans land on the water and had overcome his fear of the Woodstock sufficiently to peep from behind his tree.

He was amazed to see the three swans wade ashore, each pick up a squirrel and lift it onto its back, then do the same with a second squirrel. He was even more amazed when the swans waded into the water, swam out a little way, flapped their wings and ran along the surface before taking off heavily and flying away to the north-east. He was furious; half his enemy had escaped!

Marguerite guided the swans to land on the lagoon at Ourland in a place away from where they might be seen by humans. The squirrels hurried away, led by Wood Anemone who was the only one to have lived on that island before. Marguerite instructed the swans to return to Rowan's Pool.

"SWANS –

ONE SWAN PICK ME UP –

THREE SWANS FLY BACK TO WHERE YOU HAVE
COME FROM —
ACTION NOW — "

The swans ran across the water and took off, Marguerite
on the back of the leading swan. This is getting to be almost
a routine, she was thinking. What a wonderful way of
travelling this flying business is.

She turned her head to watch the unladen swans behind
her. There was only one other there! Away to her left, and
now well on its way towards the swannery at Abbotsbury,
was the other swan.

"THIRD SWAN —
REJOIN THE OTHERS —
ACTION NOW —
REJOIN THE OTHERS —
ACTION NOW — "

Marguerite projected her thoughts in the direction of the
single swan, now just a speck in the distance but there was
no sign that they were being received.

"TWO SWANS —
STAY TOGETHER —
FLY DOWN TO THE POOL BELOW —
ACTION NOW — "

Rowan seeing only two swans return, rushed down to the
water's edge, fearing the worst.

"Are the females all right? Meadowsweet, Bluebell . . ."

Marguerite reassured him, explained what had happened, then turned –

"TWO SWANS —

Chip was counting on his claws again.

"There are six of us and two swans, which can each carry two squirrels. So four can go but one must come back, so there must be two flights, with only three squirrels on the last flight."

Rowan tried to insist that *he* stay for the final flight but it was eventually settled by drawing twigs. Spindle and Hickory drew the short ones. They would stay, with the Woodstock to protect them.

Rowan and Marguerite were lifted onto one swan and Sycamore and Chip onto the other. Chip had hoped that he could recover his golden coin and had searched for it surreptitiously, while waiting for the swans to return, but without success.

"TWO SWANS — "

Malachite watched the birds fly off. He was not good at counting but knew there could only be two squirrels left on the island – three at the most. If they got away, so would his chance of ever becoming the Great Lord Silver. He would be the laughing stock of New America. He ordered one more charge . . .

Spindle and Hickory were sitting on the highest point of the Eyeland, Spindle keeping the Woodstock sighted on the bridge and Hickory watching the opposite bank.

When the grey attackers poured down towards the bridge, Spindle waited until the first were actually on the fallen trunk before scratching a 3 after the X on the Woodstock.

The force spiralled out and several Greys fell into the water. Spindle scratched another 3 and the mass hesitated, then turned and scrambled awkwardly up the bank. Spindle tried a 4 as they went over the top but there was no noticeable effect on the enemy and no familiar tingle in his own whiskers. The Woodstock'z power huz all gone, he thought.

The last of the wet Greys had hauled themselves ashore and climbed out of sight when a streak of blue and gold flashed past Spindle's head. A compact little bird with a long straight beak perched on the stump of a broken branch projecting from the fallen tree and peered down into the water below.

"Turn thiz way, very zlowly," Spindle said.

Hickory took one look along the opposite shoreline and did as Spindle had instructed. He saw the brilliantly coloured bird.

"What is it?" he asked in a whisper.

"Him'z a kingzfizher bird. Yew hardly ever zeez wun of them. Uz'z lucky today."

Hickory smiled to himself. He had grown fond of the ex-zervant, with his patient, helpful manner, always ready to accept whatever Life threw at him. Here were the two of them, on a tiny island, outnumbered many times over by squirrels with a totally different outlook, who were determined to kill them both, and he was saying they were lucky to see a bird!

Now he was even quoting one of their Kernels:

Zquirrelz do not live
By nutz alone. Take time off
To zeek out beauty.

Hickory looked at the bird again. The blue plumage of its back and tail was brighter than the sky above, brighter even than the reflected blue of the water below. The feathers on its underside glowed more red than gold, more gold than chestnuts. He did not even know a name for that colour.

The bird tilted off the broken branch and dived into the water, to rise a moment later with a dragonfly larva in its beak which it smashed against the tree and swallowed head first.

With a flicker of its wings it sped along the pool, a gold and blue streak above the pink and white of the lilies.

"My Wood Anemone do call kingzfizherz the birdz of happinezz," Spindle said.

Hickory's tail arched into a "question", sensed by Spindle though he was still watching the bridge.

"Her zayz that it iz no good expecting to be happy *all* the time, Life'z not like that. Now and then yew will get a glimpze of happinezz – like now and then yew will zee a kingzfizher bird. Enjoy it when yew can, her zayz."

"Kingsfishers or happiness?" Hickory asked.

"Both, yew zilly zquirrel," Spindle said, amusement and affection in his voice.

"Uz *iz* lucky then, izn't uz, Zpindle-Friend," said Hickory imitating the Ourland accent as the Greys again poured down the bank for another attack.

Hickory was alongside Spindle. "Use the Woodstock,

use the Woodstock," he shouted as the Greys streamed across the tree trunk.

"Him'z Zun-gone," said Spindle kicking the twisted stick down the bank and into the water as he leapt for a tree. Hickory leapt for another, ran up it and across a branch into Spindle's tree.

"Up to the top," he said. "Follow me."

Greys were climbing all three trees, trying to get above the two fugitives but the tree Spindle had chosen was the tallest and the two stopped just below the highest cluster of needles and turned to face downwards, one squirrel on each side of the slender trunk. The top swayed with the movements of the many Greys climbing towards them.

Lord Malachite, having learned that the Totem Stick was dead, had come out of hiding and was standing on the bridge urging others on.

"Prime territories for those who kill," he shouted. "Kill the traitor. Kill the Brown Job. Kill, kill, kill!"

"This is it, Spindle-Friend," said Hickory, twisting his tail around the trunk where it met Spindle's. The tails hooked together as a ring of savage Greys climbed ever nearer. The Red and the Grey, their tails tightly intertwined in a symbolic twist of friendship, hung by their back feet and slashed desperately at the attackers.

Grey after grey fell back, faces torn and bleeding from the claws and teeth of the squirrels above them until Malachite called a halt and the attackers withdrew down the trunk to gather round the old Lord as he gave them new instructions.

Hickory and Spindle, tails still linked, strained unsuccessfully to hear what was being said.

Soon the change of plan became apparent. Four Greys climbed the tree together, stopped just out of reach of the bloodstained claws above them and started to gnaw simultaneously through the thin trunk. Chunks of bark and splinters of wood fell among the massed Greys waiting on the Eyeland below. The scent of fresh resin drifted up to Spindle and Hickory.

"Uz do love that zmell," said Spindle.

"Take a good sniff then," replied Hickory. "It'll probably be our last. The Sun be with you."

"And with yew," said Spindle as the tree's top lurched sideways and fell into the grey mass below.

Marguerite flew back from Ourland to Rowan's Pool for the final pick-up, taking care that her instructions to the swans could not be misunderstood. As they glided in and landed on the water she knew that something terrible had happened. The swans paddled towards the Eyeland which seemed silent and deserted. Then she saw the two bodies, one red and one grey, hanging from the highest tree, their necks jammed into forks, their tails swinging in the evening breeze. High in a tree on the deserted bank of the Mainland she glimpsed a grey movement. It was another tail, that of Sitka.

Floating torpidly in the water near her was the abandoned Woodstock. Sun forbid that the Greys learn the secret of its power, she thought, and was about to direct her swan towards it, when the twisted stick, as if it was now too tired to float, tilted slowly into an upright position then sank in the deepest part of the pool. It seemed to the exhausted squirrel as if it was being drawn down by an invisible, underwater paw. Sunlight glinted on the tiny ripples created as it disappeared.

"SWANS – " she said wearily.

"SWANS –

FLY ME BACK TO THE BIG ISLAND –

ACTION NOW – "

The swans turned and once more ran down the surface of the pool, taking off and circling to gain height. Marguerite, looking down past her swan's neck, saw the mass of Greys on the ground below, heading towards the Blue Pool. Even from high above, a sense of jubilation was apparent in their movement and her anger rose.

"SWANS –

FLY LOW OVER THOSE GREY CREATURES –

ACTION NOW –

FLY STRAIGHT . . . STEADY . . .

EMPTY YOUR BOWELS –

ACTION . . . ACTION . . . ACTION . . . NOW!

FLY ME TO THE BIG ISLAND –

ACTION NOW – "

Chapter 25

Lord Malachite looked up when he heard the W-wow, W-wow, W-wow of the swans' wings overhead and watched the two white birds circle round in a wide arc, then fly in straight towards him. He was staring at the leading bird, trying to see if there was one of those hated natives clinging to its back, when a shower of stinking green dung splattered him from head to foot.

"Lord Malachite – Lord Malashite – more likely," a voice called from behind him, and he turned furiously but was unable to see which of the grinning squirrels had spoken.

"Silence!" he shouted, trying to wipe the slime from his face. "Back to your duties, all of you."

He stayed behind as the other Greys passed him, wrinkling their noses pointedly. Then he sought out one of the small pools that had formed in the remains of the many worked-out clay-pits scattered over the Great Heath. He found a pool with a fallen post reaching out into the shallow water and went along it to the end, stopped and splashed himself, washing the swan-dung from his fur and tail. When he had finished, he peered at his reflection in the water. Was that him? That old, fat squirrel staring back at him.

He sat up and looked around. The pond surface was still, except for tiny disturbances where whirly-gig beetles swam in frantic circles. Round his head damsel-flies with blue or brown bodies flitted. A pigeon coo-ed its familiar call from a pine and he suddenly felt homesick for the Tanglewood.

But no. He braced himself; there were troops dependent on him at the New Massachusetts Base, his place was there with them. He hurried off in that direction.

When he arrived, the Greys were milling about aimlessly. He climbed onto a stump and called for order. No squirrel heeded him. He called again.

"Shut it, Malashite," a Grey called. "We're all leaving. Something about this place stinks!"

The speaker flicked his tail insolently and headed off westwards, followed immediately by the others.

Lord Malachite sat on the stump until they were all gone, then hopped off in the direction of the Tanglewood, curiously light-hearted.

Burdock, the Ourland News-squirrel, was planning a field day. Even before dusk fell, she had extracted all the details of the Eyeland rescue from her mother and was preparing to spread the news across the island at first light.

TEACHING SQUIRRELS SNATCHED FROM CERTAIN DEATH

In a rescue unique in the history of squirreldom, Marguerite saves her brother and others from the raging hordes of Greys and returns with them high on a bird's back . . .

Marguerite woke to the sound of her daughter's voice and listened sadly to young Burdock telling a dramatised account of the events of the last few days, then she turned away to seek out Wood Anemone and comfort her for the loss of her life-mate, Spindle. She would probably be building a new drey in the same tree where she had had her home when she was a zervant on the island years before.

As Marguerite hopped along, Burdock's words repeated themselves in her head – high on a bird's back – high on a bird's back. The words seemed familiar, but she was sure that she could not have heard them before. No one had ever been *high on a bird's back* or even considered the possibility. She must be wrong, yet the words would not go away.

She was concentrating so hard that she nearly ran into a party of humans who had just arrived on the island by boat, hoping to see the famous red squirrels. Marguerite fled up the nearest tree, a mature birch, to their "Oo's" and "Ah's" and hid behind the trunk, catching her breath. Her claws bit deep into the silvery-white bark as she clung there. Birch-bark.

I honour birch-bark, she said to herself. *High on a bird's back – that* was the pattern of words.

Forgetting the humans, she tried Old Wally's prophecy again.

> *High on a bird's back*
> *The Island Screen. Flies stinging –*
> *The piece of the sun.*

Or it could be:

> *High on a bird's back*
> *The island's Queen. Flies stinging . . .*

If *Queen* was right then it could be:

> *High on a bird's back*
> *The island's Queen flies . . .*

But then it would be:

> *. . . Stinging . . .*
> *The piece of the sun.*

Not a lot of sense in that, although the first part felt right. Forget it; there aren't any Queens on the island now anyway, though Wally couldn't have known that when he composed his prophecy. So ran Marguerite's thoughts as the humans walked on and she resumed her search for Wood Anemone.

She found her with her twins, building a good sized drey in a pine tree, helped by Chip. She greeted them and Wood Anemone paused in her work to talk. Marguerite said how sorry she was that Spindle had been killed by the Greys, but Wood Anemone seemed to have accepted the fact easily.

"Him would have been pleezed to go like that. Him liked to help otherz, it wuz hiz whole life really. Him'z left uz two good daughterz."

She indicated the twins who were with Chip collecting moss for lining the drey. They too did not seem unhappy.

Wood Anemone continued, "Uz only regret iz that hiz body iz hanging from a tree, inztead of being cozy under the ground nourizhing won, like iz proper. But there uz iz . . ."

Chip watched until he saw the conversation cease, then hopped over.

"Quite an adventure we had . . ." then stopped, his head on one side.

"Yes," Marguerite replied, "if only we hadn't lost Spindle and Hickory, it would all have been wonderful. The flying was most exciting."

Marguerite turned to Wood Anemone, "Did you ever hear Old Wally's prophecy that starts *I honour birch-bark?*" she asked.

"Oh yez."

> *Hie honour birch-bark,*
> *The i'land'z Queen fliez, bringing*
> *The pieze of the zun.'*

"Did you say *bringing*, or *stinging?*" Marguerite asked.

"Zum zay ztinging but uz iz zure it uzed to be bringing."

"It didn't start *High on a bird's back* did it?" Marguerite asked.

"It might have done, wonze. Theze thingz changez over time, Marguerite-Friend."

> *High on a bird's back*
> *The Island's Queen flies, bringing*
> *The piece of the sun.*

"That would make some kind of sense if we knew who *the Queen* was, and what is meant by a piece of the sun," Marguerite said.

Chip was sure that *he* knew. He had heard a little about queens from Just Poplar and how beautiful they had been. The Queen in that prophecy must be his beloved

Marguerite, and the piece of the sun was that golden disc that he had so stupidly dropped in the water at Rowan's Pool. But he said nothing. He must find a way to get the gold and fulfil the prophecy. Then he would ask his Queen to be his life-mate.

"If I could get over the water I'd go back and bury Spindle," he said unexpectedly.

"Zo would uz," said Rosebay who had just joined them.

"Uz would too," said Willowherb.

As they were saying this, Sumac, on the Eyeland, was engaged in just this melancholy task.

The previous day, following the trail from the Blue Pool towards Rowan's Pool, he had heard the sounds of a group of excited Greys coming towards him and had hidden to hear what they had to say. ". . . totem stick was nasty . . . lots of curled whiskers . . . some very sick still . . . serve the Reds right . . . good native is a dead one . . . hanging there . . . covered in it he was, head to tail . . . silly old fool . . ."

Sumac heard enough to know that he was too late to be of any help. When the posse had passed, he had come out of hiding and run after them.

"Sorry to have missed the action. Only just arrived. What happened?" he asked breathlessly.

When he had heard the full story, including Malachite's humiliation, he slipped away and followed the well-beaten trail to the Eyeland Pool. It was all just as he had been told, the body of his friend Spindle was hanging from one of the island trees alongside that of Hickory, while Sitka's corpse dangled grotesquely from a tree above his own head.

Sumac climbed and dislodged Sitka's body, which fell to

the ground amid a buzzing of disturbed flies. He dragged it across the tree-trunk bridge onto the island and buried it at the foot of one of the trees, then did the same with the other two, one beneath each tree.

Judging by the accounts of the rabble he had just met, these were three fellow Sun-squirrels, two of them Silvers, who had died defending their beliefs even though it meant being branded as traitors by their fellows.

Moved by a feeling he had never before experienced, he gnawed away a small area of the pine-bark just above the ground and cut a fish symbol into the trunk of each tree.

The setting Sun lit up the bright patches of exposed wood and a tiny tear of resin oozed from the bitten bark above Spindle's grave. Sumac turned, crossed the bridge and headed back over the Great Heath towards the bulk of Screech Hill. Tumbleweed would be wondering why he had been away so long.

Chapter 26

Bluebell approached her aunt shyly. She had learned to respect Marguerite on the journey the previous year which had culminated in the battle of the Agglestone. Since Marguerite had flown in on the swan's back to rescue them, her aunt had been elevated to an almost Sun-like status in her eyes.

Marguerite looked at her niece, Rowan's daughter, waiting for her to speak, and remembering the first Bluebell who had given her life to warn the Reds of an impending attack by the Greys of the Silver Tide.

"Yes, my dear?" she said to break the ice.

"I wanted to thank you for coming and saving us, well – most of us, anyway. Did my father or mother tell you about Hickory and me?"

Marguerite shook her head.

"Well, he was a Sun-squirrel like us, even if he was a Silver, and I loved him. I can't bear to think of him hanging in a tree to be eaten by maggots. Is there any way we can go back and bury him?" she asked.

Marguerite felt a surge of love towards her kin-squirrel. Bluebell was ready to risk her own life just to bury a dead

Grey who she had cared for. This was the second time in two days that squirrels had wanted to return to the Mainland that she had thought they had left for ever.

"Leave it with me, my dear, I'll think about it and see if we can do anything."

She went to look for Chip but found her son, Oak, first.

"Is it true what Burdock is saying about you and the swans?" he asked.

"Mostly, but Burdock does like to add bits here and there to make a more dramatic story. She says more squirrels listen to her if she does that."

"What's it like flying? Nothing exciting seems to happen here on Ourland."

Marguerite outlined her adventures; the balloon flight, crossing the sea on a broken oar held by a dolphin, the rescue of Finisterre and the flight home on the swan's back, not forgetting the lifting of Rowan's party from the Eyeland.

"Wow! All that in two days. Nothing ever happens here, I wish I could go to the Mainland."

Sycamore joined them.

"Oak-Friend," he said, all his previous sullenness gone. "You should have been with us – did we have some fun?"

"I wish I had been," Oak replied.

"Marguerite."

She turned to see Rowan, with Meadowsweet beside him.

Meadowsweet spoke first. "Our Bluebell says that you are going to get her back to the Eyeland to bury Hickory. Is this true?"

"She asked me if it was possible and I said I would think about it. Rosebay and Willowherb want to go back as well; even Chip says he would. Now I've got Sycamore getting Oak wanting to go. I'd have thought that they would want to stay here, where it's peaceful."

"They're all young," said Rowan. "They need adventure, something to make their blood flow, give them a tingle."

"I'd have thought, except perhaps for Oak, they would have had enough. I have."

"Yes, but you're older. All youngsters need adventures and challenges; they get bored and troublesome otherwise."

"Should we let them go back, if that's what they want?"

"If it was me, you'd have a job to stop me," said Rowan. "If they do go back to bury Spindle, Hickory and Sitka, I'd be pleased. I don't like the idea of them all hanging there. And the youngsters might be able to find out what the Greys are up to."

"But how? Remember Ourland here is an island in the sea. There's no tree-trunk making a bridge from here to the Mainland."

"That never seems to bother you, Marguerite, you've crossed four times, a different way each time. You'll think of something. When you do, I think we should encourage them."

"But it could be dangerous."

"True, but life always has been dangerous for squirrels, that's what keeps us alert – and alive. You'll think of something. *If you think you can . . .*"

*

Either by coincidence or Sun-plan, the dolphins swam in on the evening tide and thought-called to Marguerite as she sat looking up at the giant squirrel that Larch and his family had carved. Some idle tail-wag of a youngster had bitten the tufted ears off, and cut circles round its eyes, so that it appeared to be wearing those glass things that some humans hooked over their ears.

"Marguerite-Friend," Lundy called. "We have come so that Finisterre can thank you for your help. He is much better and we have all recovered from our ordeal. It seems much more than three days ago. How are you? The swans evidently brought you back safely."

Marguerite projected her thoughts and told of the incidents on the flight and the loss of the three Sun-squirrels.

"If we can ever help you, let us know. We owe Finisterre's life to you and your friends."

"We were glad to be able to repay you for all you have done for us in the past," Marguerite said, "but there *is* a little help you could give – if you are not too busy now."

"Our patrol is being swum by others until Finisterre is fully recovered. How can we help?"

"There are squirrels, five altogether, who want to go back to the Mainland to finish off some business there and find what the Greys are up to now. Could you take them?"

"Glad to. When do they want to go?"

"They could be ready at first light."

"Do they want a boat, or can we carry them on sticks in our mouths, that would be easiest. It's not far this time."

"Sticks would be fine."

They discussed the finer details and then Malin asked how the five would return.

"I hadn't thought of that," Marguerite admitted, "everything is happening so fast."

"It's the New Moon in two weeks time. We'll pick up your scouting patrol from the same beach as we drop them at, on New-Moon night. If they're not there we'll come back each New Moon until they come. Rely on us. Until the morning then."

The three dark bodies swam out into the tideway and disappeared under the water.

There was only an hour of daylight left. Marguerite ran off to find Burdock.

"Can you get a message to Sycamore, Bluebell, Rosebay and Willowherb tonight?" she asked breathlessly.

"I'm a News-squirrel, not a Post-squirrel, but yes, I'm sure I can, Marguerite-Ma. What's the message?"

"The dolphins will pick up five squirrels at Pottery Point at first light tomorrow to take them to the Mainland to bury Spindle and the two Greys and to find out what the other Greys are up to."

"You only gave me four names; who's the other?"

"Chip. *I'll* tell him."

"Oak – your son – wanted to go!"

Marguerite thought quickly, one extra squirrel would not make the patrol too large, and Oak needed the experience. "If you can find him, tell him to be ready as well. And . . ."

Burdock stood expectantly.

"A True Message this time. No elaboration . . ."

"Marguerite-Ma – as if I would!"

It was one of those late-summer mornings when autumn

lets you know it is not far away. A certain chill was in the air, and a smell of ripeness, with just a hint of decay, drifted through the woodland to tickle the nostrils of early risers.

At Pottery Point it seemed that the whole squirrel population of Ourland was there to see the patrol leave. The dolphins were just off-shore, each holding a length of driftwood sideways in their mouths. They swam in small circles picking up the sense of squirrelation that was coming from the massed ranks on the beach.

The six squirrel scouts were on the beach, watched by envious youngsters, most of whom would have given their whiskers, if not their tails, to have been able to join the patrol. Marguerite was clearly in charge, pairing the squirrels and allocating each pair to a dolphin.

"Oak, you go with Bluebell, swim out to Malin – that's the biggest dolphin. Chip, you and Sycamore swim out to Lundy; and Rosebay, you go with Willowherb and climb onto Finisterre's stick. You can all swim, can't you? The water's quite warm and you will dry off quickly when you're ashore. Good luck!"

The remaining squirrels watched the scouting party disappear into the early haze as the dolphins swam up the channel. Just Poplar and Clover came to Marguerite's side.

"Can we have a word with yew when the otherz have left?" Just Poplar said quietly.

Chapter 27

"Marguerite," Just Poplar said when only the three of them were left on the beach. "Who iz the zelected Leader of Ourland?"

Marguerite immediately realised the import of the question and felt a rush of concern and regret. She had organised all of this activity without any reference to the Leader, the Tagger or any of the other senior squirrels.

"Oh, Poplar, I know what you are going to say and I am sorry. I just got swept along. All of those young squirrels wanted to go and bury Spindle and when the dolphins offered to take them . . ."

Her voice trailed away. She realised that she was speaking her defence and may have to do so before the full Council if Clover accused her of acting incorrectly. Having been Tagger herself, she knew that she had done just that.

Clover saw the contrite look on her friend's face and reached out a paw.

"It's all right, Marguerite-Friend, we'll call it 'acting on your own initiative'."

Initiative
Is a name for successful
Disobedience.

"Let's hope that the patrol are able to carry out their mission and return safely. They're all fairly young."

"I thinkz it will be good for them," said Just Poplar. "Uz'd have liked to go zcouting on the Mainland when uz wuz young. Too old now though. Being Leader iz tiring enough with all theze troublezome youngzterz. Do yew know what zome did yezterday? . . ."

The dolphins swam steadily westwards, keeping to the deeper waters. Malin explained to Chip, who could follow Dolphin-think, that this way would avoid the mudflats and the boggy harbour shores and they would land at Tallships Point beyond the Long Island.

The squirrels' fur was dry again by the time they reached Tallships. The dolphins cruised along, watching the shore and looking for the best place to land the scouts. There was a Man-drey on the point and, to the south of this, two oak trees grew right on the water's edge, with their roots washed out from under them by the sea so that they appeared to stand on many legs.

"Those are a good landmark," Malin indicated to Chip. "This is where we'll pick you up again at dawn after the night of the New Moon." They turned in towards the beach as Chip thanked them.

Rosebay helped her sister Willowherb, who she knew was a poor swimmer and frightened of water. Wet through once again, the squirrels climbed the low gravelly cliff and sat in the heather watching the dolphins swim down-channel.

"We're on our own now," said Oak the Wary, "the sooner we can get to those trees, the better."

On Ourland Marguerite, Poplar and Clover climbed to the top of the bank and found Rowan and Meadowsweet waiting there.

"We've not really been introduced," Rowan said to Poplar. "I am Rowan the Bold and this is Meadowsweet Rowan's-love. Our daughter, Bluebell, is one of those who has just gone with the dolphins."

"Thiz iz Clover," Poplar said, "but yew will remember her from when yew were all at the Blue Pool, her iz now the Tagger of Ourland, and uz'z Juzt Poplar, the Leader. Uz iz zorry that uz haven't welcomed yew before. Zo much zeemz to be happening all at wonze! Yew'r zizter iz highly thought of here."

Hearing this, Marguerite smiled and her tail rose noticeably.

"Uz expectz that yew will want to rezd after all yew have been through," Poplar continued.

Rowan replied, "I – we are fine. We were hoping to find something to occupy us. We are both experienced teachers and enjoy that. Can you use us in any way?"

"There iz a lot of thingz not right here at prezent. Perhapz yew, zeeing it with new eyeze, zo to zpeak, can zee what needz to be done and teach uz what to do."

Sitting in the areas flattened by the tents of the departed boy scouts, the five squirrels held an impromptu meeting in the grass behind Pottery Point to analyse the problems that were afflicting the squirrel population of the island.

Most seemed to have grown out of boredom. With an abundance of food and no predators, there was nothing to keep the youngsters on their claws.

"That party that went to the Mainland this morning—" Clover said, "if we could organise such scouting patrols regularly, they would provide adventure for the youngsters."

"Would your dolphins help us again?" she asked Marguerite.

"They're not really *my* dolphins, but yes, I think they would."

Meadowsweet said, "All the scouts would need to be taught how to look after themselves and survive in hostile country, *that* could be a job for Rowan and me. We know quite a bit about the Greys as well as about squirrelship and survival."

"We must put these ideas to the Council," said Clover.

"What Council?" said Poplar. "It'z zuppozed to include all the zquirrelz but hardly any com'z nowadayz."

"I don't think you can have a Council with all the squirrels, like we used to at the Blue Pool," said Rowan. "You probably need to have a Council of just a few senior ones and make each of those a guardian of different things."

"Zum zquirrel would have to be in charge," said Poplar. "A zort of King like uz father wuz."

"The problem then, was that *he* made all the decisions, no other squirrel's views mattered," Marguerite reminded him.

"Uz knowz that. That'z why uz abolished it all. Uz wuz King vor a few minutez, remember. That kind of power corruptz. Yew'd make a good Queen, Marguerite-Friend, it would be hard to corrupt yew."

"Me? I'd never be a Queen!"

The scouting party had paused in a tree overlooking some wide fields. So far it had been easy. Humans had made a wooden walk-way through the marshier places and the squirrels had scurried along that, then taken to the trees, mostly oak and birch, all close enough together for them to run and leap from one to the next.

In a state of high exhilaration, they eventually slowed down and halted to regain their breath. A noise like a wasp immediately drew their attention towards a human, tiny in the distance, bent down at the foot of a tree and holding something red. The wasp-sound changed slightly, held steady for a minute, then the human stood up and stepped hurriedly back. The squirrels watched in horror as the distant tree lurched over and fell to the ground. The swish of its leaves and the crunch as the trunk hit the earth reached the squirrels a second later.

Oak, shocked, said, "We must move on, this is a dangerous place."

Chapter 28

Marguerite was with her old friend on a branch outside Wood Anemone's new drey, talking of the time when they had been forced to flee from Ourland together. She wanted to know about the moon mushrooms but felt that it was better to raise the subject obliquely and not rush straight on to it.

"You were called Woodlouse then," she said.

"Zo uz wuz! It do zeem a long time ago."

"It *was* a long time ago," said Marguerite, "and your Spindle was called Spider in those days."

"The Royalz alwayz called zervantz after creepy-crawliez, them did it to keep uz in uz placez, them zaid."

Mention of Spindle made both squirrels think of his body hanging from the Eyeland tree and each wondered how the scouts were progressing with their mission. Five days had passed since Wood Anemone had said farewell to her twin daughters. She had since realised that if they did not come back from what could be a hazardous journey, her family line would end.

"Uz wizhez that uz had only let won go with yew'r dolphinz," she said to Marguerite.

"You know that Rosebay and Willowberb are always together. Sun-knows what will happen when one chooses a mate. It'll be 'take me, take my sister'."

"Marguerite!" said Wood Anemone, shocked at the suggestion. "That'z the zort of thing the Royalz did."

"Poplar suggested that I should be Queen," Marguerite confided to her friend.

"Yew zhould be; yew would make a good Queen," replied Wood Anemone bluntly. "Yew iz vull of good ideaz and all the zquirrelz lovez and rezpectz yew."

"Some call me Miss Hoity-Toity," Marguerite said ruefully.

"If uz hearz any doing that, uz'll pull their tailz," said Wood Anemone. "Yew ignore them. Yew'll make uz a good Queen."

"I'm not going to be Queen. It was only something that Poplar said."

The two sat in comfortable silence enjoying the early September sunshine and watching the people who passed underneath. The human youngsters seemed to have suddenly stopped coming to the island. Only a few days before they had been there in great numbers, now the humans they saw were mostly older and in pairs, or were those men who wore the "Acorn" badge on their green coverings.

"How many squirrels were on the island before we came?" Marguerite asked.

"Yew knowz uz can't count like yew do'z, but there were a 'lot' of Royalz and 'lotz' of zervantz."

"Did there ever get to be too many?"

"Oh no. Uz zaw to that," said Wood Anemone enigmatically.

"How do you mean?" Marguerite asked.

"Uz'z zorry, Marguerite-Friend, uz can't zay."

"Come on, of course you can. We're friends. Whatever it is, you can tell me."

"Uz can't. Uz zwore to keep the zecret. Uz can only talk about it with a King of a Queen, or with their matez. Uz zwore not to tell otherz."

"Tell others what?"

"How to stop zquirrelz breeding too vazd. With the King and the Kingz-mate Zun-gone, only *uz* knowz. Only Woodlouze knowz."

"The Kings-mate was saying something like that to me when she was dying. *She* said, 'Woodlouse knows'."

"What elze did her zay?"

"How the mushrooms of the moon can control breeding. I want you to tell me everything you know. It's very important."

"Uz can't tell yew, unlezz yew'z a Queen."

Nothing Marguerite said could get the old zervant to tell her any more.

The scouts were resting in a hedgerow tree.

"Alert everyone, dogs in sight," Oak said quietly.

They peered between the leaves. Two brown and white dogs had just wriggled under a gate on the far side of the field and were sniffing their way along the hedge. Two men appeared at the gate and the squirrels watched them open it and come through. Each man was carrying a short stick under his right arm with the thinnest end pointing towards the ground.

"Guns," said Bluebell. "Rowan-Pa told me about them.

He saw them when he was on climbabout. Humans use them to kill animals and birds."

"Squirrels?" asked Sycamore.

"I don't think so," said Bluebell, "but you can never tell with humans; they're so unpredictable."

"Keep still and don't show yourselves," said Oak the Wary, parting the leaves carefully.

The dogs were sniffing their way in zigzags across the field when a covey of partridge, two adults and eight young birds, burst into the air and flew towards the squirrels.

The men raised the guns and fired four times. The squirrels instinctively ducked with each report, then ducked again as shot rattled like hail stones on the leaves.

A gap appeared in the arc of birds as two dropped in tumbled heaps of feathers to be seized by the dogs. Two others glided awkwardly into the hedge bottom where they lay, struggling pitiably, the larger of the two trying to escape on its one unbroken leg. The survivors of the family cleared the hedge and dropped into the field behind.

A dog found one of the injured birds and carried it, still cheeping, to the taller of the two men, who pulled its neck. The cheeping stopped. The man grinned at his companion as he put the limp body into the bag slung across his shoulder.

"No squirrel move," whispered Oak.

The shocked squirrels watched the last injured partridge, its feathers stained with blood, fluttering feebly as its life drained away and the brightness faded from its eyes.

Its brothers and sisters scurried noisily along the dead leaves beneath the hedge, then rose again and flew off behind the cover of the bushes.

A dog found the dead bird, carried it to the man, received a pat on the head and returned to the tree, where it sat looking up into the branches. It whined softly and the other dog joined it. The men walked across to the tree and peered up.

A gust of wind caught Willowherb's tail and one man, seeing the movement, raised his gun and pointed it at her. She sat petrified with fear.

"Keep very still," Oak whispered.

The second man joined his companion and they appeared to be arguing. At last the other man lowered the gun, whistled to the dogs to follow him and the two men walked down the hedgerow in the direction that the partridges had flown.

"That was close," said Oak. "This Mainland is a dangerous place. And I still don't know whether humans kill squirrels."

Chapter 29

Marguerite left Wood Anemone and wandered up the island, knowing that her friend held the secret of why Ourland had not been overrun with squirrels in the past, and frustrated because she would not, or could not, confide in her. The secret was in those Moon Mushrooms, whatever they were.

"Greetings, Marguerite the Seeker."

Marguerite looked up to see Heather Treetops and Chestnut the Doubter. She had forgotten that "the Seeker" was her tag. Somehow tagging seemed to be losing its importance. Many of the youngsters had not yet been given tags and those that had, largely ignored them. Youngsters were as often as not referred to by their father's name. She could not remember the tag, if he had one, of Elm Larchson.

She greeted the two formally in the old way, and accepted Chestnut's invitation to see their Woodstock plantation.

In that quiet copse, away from any Man-tracks, Heather and Chestnut had dug up more young honeysuckle plants from other places, replanted them near the roots of several hazel bushes, and were training the growing woodbine shoots around the hazel saplings. Evidence of the earlier raid by idle youngsters was to be seen in the piles of creeper stems, bitten into short lengths, which lay nearby.

Chestnut saw Marguerite looking at these, and said, "I hope for all our sakes that we don't need these Woodstocks too soon. Those Sun-damned young idiots set us back a whole year."

"I hope we never need them," said Marguerite.

"So do we, but I don't trust Grey squirrels not to try and come here, and it is best to be ready," Chestnut said.

> To ensure a Peace
> A wise squirrel will always
> Prepare for a War.

"I don't know that Kernel," said Marguerite. "Who taught you that?"

"We made it up," Chestnut replied. "Do you like it?"

"I think it's a sound idea," said Marguerite, "but it's a pity we have to have words like War and Peace."

She left them and wandered on, her mind back on how to persuade Wood Anemone to reveal her secret. Perhaps if she spelt out the importance of it all to her friend, she would tell. The ex-zervant was no fool.

"Wood Anemone, you *must* tell me about the Mushrooms of the Moon! You don't know how important it is!"

Marguerite went on to tell her friend all about Chip's calculations and his and her concerns about an over-abundance of squirrels on the island.

"But uz *can't* tell yew," Wood Anemone replied. "Uz zwore on uz life and the livez of uz family and uz friendz, not to tell. Only to Kingz and Queenz and their matez.

"Uz could tell yew if yew wuz a Queen," she added, watching Marguerite's reaction.

"You know how I feel about that," Marguerite replied.

"I know how yew feelz about the zecret of the Moon Mushroomz, too," said Wood Anemone. "Yew would make uz a good Queen. Thiz plaze needz won, even uz can zee that!"

The scouting party had escaped from two more dogs and a farmyard cat, had spent uncomfortable nights without proper shelter and had at last reached the North-east Wood near the Blue Pool. They came through the trees cautiously, unsure of their reception from any Greys that might be there. They need not have worried; all the dreytels were empty and cold. They checked each one, but there was no sign of current occupation and no recent scent of Greys.

They circled the Blue Pool, calm in the autumn sunshine, and they fed well at the Hazel Copse, although the nuts were not fully developed. The small nearly-formed kernels were extra tasty and sweet.

The Pool area held mixed memories for them all, except Sycamore, but even he was taken by its beauty and could at last understand why it meant so much to those squirrels on Ourland who had once lived in this demesne.

They briefly visited the empty and forlorn dreys on Steepbank that had once been their homes, then headed towards Rowan's Pool. At the Dogleg Field, Bluebell looked at the twins and said, 'Anyone fancy a ride on a horse?' and smiled.

"Uz iz ztaying on the ground," Rosebay replied, followed by Willowherb's, "On the ground, uz too."

The squirrels dodged amongst the tall thistles as they crossed the field, unseen by the chestnut and the piebald horse and when the roadway was clear, crossed that and were onto the Great Heath.

"Go carefully," said Oak. "It was near here where we met that fox."

They went slowly, scenting the air every few yards, but they were in the belt of trees near Rowan's Pool before they found fresh scent and Fox-dread affected them. Sycamore, who had never smelt fox before, was most affected. They all had to sit in a tree while he composed himself, waiting for the coldness and shivering to stop.

They could not see any sign of the fox below but they moved through the treetops until they reached the edge of the Pool, where they expected to see the three bodies hanging. There were none.

"The vox muzd have vound them," said Rosebay.

"Vound by the vox," repeated Willowherb.

"Voxes – foxes don't climb trees," Oak said.

"Good thing too," said Sycamore.

They descended slowly, watching all about, then, when they were sure that no fox was near, the six squirrels dropped to the ground and scampered across the fallen tree to the Eyeland.

At the foot of each pine was a neat mound of earth and, abov̩ each mound, a ⌖ symbol had been cut into the bark of the tree.

"Some Sun-sqirrel has been here before us." Oak stated the obvious.

"And scattered the ground-drey," said Bluebell. "Though the Greys may have done that. I wonder which grave is my Hickory's."

Chip was at the water's edge where the swans had waded ashore. He could see his gold coin in the now clear water but decided that he would not mention it just yet.

"If there's nothing more to do, we should start back. There's still an hour of daylight left," said Oak.

Chip looked round. "I think we should stay the night; we can sleep safely in the trees here. It would be indecent to dash away having come so far and we'll be safe here if that fox is still about."

Chapter 30

Chip was awake at first light and, leaving the other squirrels dozing in the Eyeland trees, he slipped down to the water's edge. From the shore he could see a glinting of gold on the bottom but when he waded in the water again turned milky with particles of disturbed clay. By feeling around with his feet, he located the coin and scrabbled it onto the land. He picked it up in his teeth and was carrying it to the foot of one of the trees.

"Chip, look out, the fox!"

Chip turned and saw the red-brown fur of a large animal crossing the bridge. Still holding the coin in his mouth he leapt for the trunk and ran up it as the white teeth snapped at his tail.

"Sun, that was close!"

Marguerite had, for the time being, given up trying to persuade Wood Anemone to tell her the secret that she felt was so vital to the future of the Ourland squirrels. She was in the Palm Tree Valley, thinking. Wood Anemone was getting older, as indeed they all were. Supposing she were to die and take the secret with her. The knowledge of the moon mushrooms could be lost for ever. It was clear that the ex-zervant wanted to force her friend to become Queen.

A Queen was not necessarily bad because she was called a Queen. What was bad was when the privilege was abused. Supposing that somehow or other she should become Queen, could she hold that position without becoming corrupted by power? Who could tell? The only way would be to hold a Tail-poll each year to ask the squirrels to confirm that they still wanted her to be Queen. That would work. Now, if she was going to ensure the safe future of the island she must find a way to become "Queen".

Marguerite moved up the valley, foraging, not thinking much about the direction she was taking. At the valley head she went through the bracken and the scattered pines to the cliff-edge, feeling that if she could talk with the dolphins they would help her clarify her thoughts. She climbed one of the tallest trees and projected her thoughts seawards, but no matter how hard she tried, there was no response. She consoled herself with the thought that the dolphins must be too far away but were due back in a few days, at New Moon, to return the scouts to the island; and dolphins were always on time.

She recalled what Malin had said when they had first met off Finfast Point and Lundy had repeated:

> *Punctuality*
> *Is vital. Others' time wasted,*
> *Is stolen by you*
> *And can never be returned.*
> *Lost minutes sink for ever.*

That was it. It started as a Kernel but had two more lots of seven sounds. Did dolphins call these "Kernels", or did they have some other, perhaps fishy, name for them? Life was full of questions.

On the shore below her she could see a swan. She watched it for a while, remembering the exhilarating feeling of being "high on a bird's back".

> *High on a bird's back*
> *The Island's Queen flies – bringing*
> *The Peace of the Sun.*

Peace – not *piece*. That was it – *now* the prophecy made sense. If she was the Island's Queen, she had flown high on a bird's back and if she was Queen then Wood Anemone could tell her the secret and there would be the Sun's Peace on the island for ever.

Life was full of answers too, if you thought hard enough. Marguerite suddenly felt very humble.

She looked down at the swan again; there was something wrong with the way it was sitting on the beach. It just did not look right.

Marguerite thought briefly about rushing off to tell Wood Anemone that she had decided to see if the others would accept her as Queen, when she saw the swan shake its head feebly and rest its neck on the gravelly beach. Something was definitely wrong. She climbed down the pine trunk and made her way towards it.

As she got nearer she saw that the normally gleaming white feathers were streaked with some black substance which was also around the swan's beak. It had obviously been trying to clean itself.

Marguerite looked at the bird closely, but could not be sure if it was one of those which had flown her and her friends to the island, but this did not matter. She wanted to help but did not know what to do; the swan looked very sick.

She went up the bank and across the island to look for Clover and the two ex-princesses, Voxglove and Cowzlip, to see if any of these Carers would know how to help the stricken swan.

They could suggest nothing but to ensure that food was brought to it each day and, with the Sun's help, it might recover.

The scouts huddled together in one of the trees on the Eyeland watching the fox waiting patiently below.

"I'm hungry," said Sycamore, having seen that there were no cones whatsoever left on any of the three trees.

"Zo's that vox," said Rosebay.

"That vox iz too," said Willowherb.

"We can't stay here," said Oak in a whisper, as though the fox could understand his words. "We must get across to the land and escape or we won't get back in time to meet the dolphins, especially if we run into more trouble. We must allow at least six days."

They discussed possibilities. Unless a human came to frighten the fox away, or he gave up and left, there seemed only one solution. They would have to leap into the water and swim across to the land, hoping to reach safety there before the fox caught any of them.

They came slowly down to the lower branches, staying just out of reach of the animal prowling below them, and each planned a route along a branch. Chip held his coin tightly between his teeth.

Willowherb whispered to her sister, "Uz'z zcared of the vox, uz iz. Uz can't jump that far and uz can't zwim vast."

"Yew go virzt, uz'z be behind yew."

Oak shouted "Now," and five of the squirrels ran along branches, leapt out into the pool and swam towards the opposite shore. The fox sprang after them and swam strongly towards Willowherb, his mouth only just behind the terrified squirrel's tail.

Rosebay, who had stayed in the tree, ran and leapt onto the swimming fox's head, clawing at his eyes. The two sank in a flurry of scrabbling and splashing as the other squirrels reached the far shore and climbed a tree to safety. Chip, the coin still tight between his teeth, spluttering and coughing awkwardly as he did so.

"Where'z Rozebay, where'z Rozebay," wailed Willowherb.

They watched in horror as the writhing bodies surfaced and sank again, then resurfaced.

The fox swam back to the Eyeland carrying the limp and lifeless body of Rosebay.

"Don't look," said Bluebell to Willowherb as the sound of bones being crunched reached their ears.

Chapter 31

Between the many discussion meetings that were being held, Marguerite did what little she could for the sick swan.

Wood Anemone addressed a special Council Meeting which she had asked Just Poplar to call.

"Yellow squirrelz," she had said. "Uz huz lived on the Mainland for more than a year. When uz left Ourland there wuz a King here, Poplar'z vather, and uz knowz that Poplar won't mind uz zaying that zum of the thingz hiz vather did wuz not *good* thingz. Now, when uz comez back there iz no King and yew iz all trying to do thingz like they wuz done at the Blue Pool. Yew can zee az well az uz can, that it izn't working. Thiz i'land needz a King – or a Queen. Zo uz propozez that Marguerite should be our Queen."

There was a silence as each squirrel considered the likely consequences if the proposal was approved.

"Long live Queen Marguerite," Just Poplar said, at last.

"Wait please," Marguerite held up her paw, "there might be some other squirrel more worthy than me."

"Any other propozalz?" Poplar glowered round at the assembly.

"No? Long live Queen Marguerite. The meeting iz yewrz, Ma'am."

"Please. Do not call me Ma'am. I am Marguerite still, and I accept *only* if you promise to hold a Tail-poll at each Harvest Celebration to see if you would rather have another squirrel to be Queen – or King."

"Long live Queen Marguerite."

Marguerite smiled round at her friends. "I declare today to be a Sun-day in celebration." Then she slipped away to take food to the swan.

"It's your fault," Sycamore said to Chip. "If you hadn't made us stay last night so that you could get your Sun-damned gold thing, Rosebay would still be with us."

"That's hardly fair," said Bluebell. "We all decided to stay, you don't know what foxes are going to do. It might have attacked us last night."

"Voxes iz horrid, eating other animalz," said Willowherb.

"That's not fair either," Bluebell responded. "That's how foxes live. A fox has to do what a fox has to do. Think how lucky you are being a squirrel; at least your nuts don't try and run away when you are eating them."

"Shut up, Bluebell," said Oak. "You're not helping. Oh Sun, it's back.'"

The fox had finished his meal and had come to the foot of the tree where they were sitting. Now he was watching them eagerly, his pink tongue lolling out of the side of his mouth. Willowherb was sure she could see blood on the fox's lips.

Marguerite had asked Rowan and Meadowsweet to take over teaching Kernels, Traditions and Manners to the young squirrels and also to train them in wood-craft and survival. Having seen the difference that a few days of Mainland adventure had had on Sycamore she was beginning to formulate an idea that might stop the mindless behaviour of the island youngsters.

She had already asked Just Poplar to be Guardian of Justice on Ourland, and had made him swear to live up to his Tag at all times and never let anyone, especially herself, influence his judgement.

Let Justice be done,
In every squirrel's case,
Though the sky may fall.

"If expediency affects justice, then we are not worthy to govern," she had told him.

She appointed Chestnut and Heather to be Guardians of Defence and asked Clover to relinquish the post of Tagger which was no longer relevant, and help Voxglove and Cowzlip do all they could to help sick and elderly squirrels. Clover agreed readily.

Then Queen Marguerite sought out Wood Anemone.

"Now, Wood Anemone-Friend, or should I call you Woodlouse? I want you to tell me all about the Mushrooms of the Moon. And don't you dare call me Ma'am!"

They brushed whiskers and hugged one another.

212

"Can uz be yewr zervant?" Wood Anemone asked.

"No, you can be uz – my friend and companion. I do get lonely on my own. Now, please, tell me about those Mushrooms."

The scouts in the tree were whispering together again.

"If we go back the way we came, we have to come down out of the trees before we have gone very far," Oak said. "We might be able to circle round and go back another way whilst staying safely off the ground."

"If we split up, we can see how big this wood is and whether there is a safe route out," said Sycamore. "Then meet back here."

They each went off in a different direction, Chip lodging his coin in a fork of the tree before he went. The fox prowled about below, keeping one or other of the squirrels always in his sight.

An hour later they were back, Chip returning last. He looked for his coin; it was not in the fork where he had left it, but lay on the ground near the fox's feet. It could not have fallen by itself.

"Who threw down my gold thing?" he asked.

Every squirrel was looking away and none answered.

"More important than that, is there a safe way out of this wood?" Oak asked.

Each scout reported that they had come to the edge of the copse and would have had to drop to the ground before getting to the next clump of trees.

"We're trapped here then until the fox goes away," said Bluebell. "At least there's plenty of things for us to eat – not like on the Eyeland."

Sycamore said, "When I was on the Eyeland with you before, you had a Woodstock thing. I saw one of those growing over there."

They followed him to the edge of the copse where a tangle of honeysuckle enmeshed the top of a hazel bush. Lower down they could see the unmistakable bulge of a Woodstock – but it was low down, possibly within reach of a hungry fox.

"I'll try and cut it out of the stem," said Sycamore. "Call me if the fox comes too close." He ducked as a large brown and yellow insect flew past his head towards a hollow tree across the glade. "Did you see the size of that wasp?' he asked. 'It was enormous!"

Chip edged along the branch towards the disconsolate Willowherb.

"I'm sorry about Rosebay," he said. "But it was a brave thing that she did."

"Her did a brave thing," replied Willowherb.

"Look out," called Bluebell as the fox leapt up at Sycamore but fell just short. He leapt again but could not quite reach the young squirrel as he bit and gnawed at the hazel stem.

When Sycamore's teeth were aching, he handed over to Oak. Between them they cut through below the Woodstock, the fox all the while leaping up at them in vain.

Bluebell and Chip finished cutting the Woodstock clear, and together they pulled it to the top of the mass of honeysuckle, where it lay on the tangle of fine stems while they peeled off the bark and cut the now familiar numbers:

1 Z 7 4 5 6 7 10 X .

The fox prowled back and forth below them.

"What number shall I use?" Bluebell asked.

"Enuff to kill the nazty thing," said Willowherb but the others disagreed.

"A 3 or a 4 should curl its whiskers and stop it chasing us," said Bluebell. "He was only being a fox. And foxes eat squirrels when they can. That's how things are."

She sighted the Woodstock at the fox and scratched a 3 .

There was a yelp of surprise but the fox only pawed at his face, shook his head, and continued his prowling below them.

"Try a 4 ," suggested Oak. This was no more effective. That fox has tough whiskers," Bluebell remarked as another and another of the big wasps flew past towards the distant hollow tree. "Try a 5 ."

None of the numbers proved effective against the fox. He yelped a little each time the Woodstock was used, but his whiskers stayed as straight as pine needles.

Sycamore was watching the yellow and brown insects as they zoomed past.

"I wonder if those big-wasps have big stings," he said.

"Why," asked Oak.

"We might be able to get them to sting the fox," he replied.

"You won't get me poking a twig in their nest," said Oak. "You can try if you like."

"No, I wondered if the Woodstock Force might stir them up," said Sycamore. "We could do that from here; we're a safe distance away."

They all agreed it was worth a try but that one squirrel would have to tease the fox to keep it near the big-wasps' nest while the others stayed well back. Bluebell drew the short twig and lightly ran along a branch and leapt across to the lower branches of the hollow tree.

From there she chattered insults at the fox, who had followed her. She was careful to keep just out of his reach.

"You're in the way of the Woodstock," Oak called to her. "You'll have to go higher."

The fox sat and watched her climb.

Oak aimed at the hole in the tree and scratched a 𝟤. There was a low rumble from within the tree and the squirrels saw a cloud of big-wasps pour angrily from the hole. The fox turned and ran, yelping and biting at his flanks as hornet after hornet caught up with him and forced their sharp stings through his fur. The yelping faded into the distant sounds of the wood.

Bluebell, unthinking of the danger to her, had watched the scene until she realised that one of the big-wasps had seen her and was coming to attack. She leapt for the next tree, the big-wasp just behind her, raced through the branches and into the next tree. She could still hear the whir of its wings behind her head and ran on towards the pool.

At the last tree she jumped for the water, submerging and coming up under a lily leaf near the shore where her feet were able to touch bottom. Here she stayed, holding the leaf above her head until the frustrated hornet gave up the search and returned to its nest. She crawled out to dry, her teeth chattering with fear, relief and cold.

As soon as the fox was gone and the big-wasps had returned to their nest, Chip climbed down and rushed across the leaf litter to recover the coin. The others followed the direction that Bluebell had taken and found her on the poolside.

"That was well done," said a voice from behind them, and they turned to see a grey squirrel's face grinning at them.

"Zumac! It'z yew!"

"Bluebell, Willowherb . . . where's Rosebay?"

The Grey and the two Reds brushed whiskers, then Bluebell, her chattering gone in the delight at meeting an old friend, introduced Oak and Sycamore.

"Sumac is a Sun-squirrel," Bluebell explained. "Rowan-Pa said he was his best pupil ever."

Sumac looked suitably modest, then asked again about Rosebay.

They told their story and Sumac silently embraced Willowherb.

"Was it you who buried . . . ?" Bluebell's voice trailed away.

"Hickory and Sitka, and your father, Spindle. Yes they're all nourishing trees now, as your Farewell Kernel teaches."

Oak the Wary was listening to Bluebell and Sumac. He was uneasy about the way she was treating him as a trusted friend; after all he was a Grey. He may profess to be a Sun-squirrel but Oak was not going to give him a chance to learn the secret of the Woodstock. He left them exchanging news and slipped back to where the weapon had been dropped when they had followed Bluebell.

Chip was there with his gold disc.

"We must hide the Woodstock," Oak said. "There are Greys about."

"Change the figures," Chip suggested, "Then it won't matter if they *do* find it."

"Watch in case the fox comes back, and listen for the big-wasps."

Oak bit into the wood, tasting the sweet sap of the hazel. His sharp teeth rapidly changed the **1** into **◁**, the **2** into **◪**, the **3** into **ß** and the **4** into **⊕** The **5** became **⊟**, the **6** : **⊟** the **7** : **⅍** and the **10** : **⊕**. Finally he made the **X** look like **⊠**, and as he did this he felt the power drain from the Woodstock as the life had drained from the shot partridge.

"Where shall we hide it?" he asked Chip.

Together they pushed the inert stick end-first into the mound of pine needles covering a wood-ants' nest, brushing the ants from their fur and scampering away before they could be bitten.

"It'll be a brave Grey who gets that out, even if they did find it," said Oak.

When they rejoined the others they heard Bluebell say, "Thank you, Sumac-friend. Where is Tumbleweed?"

"She should be here soon. She has been helping old Malachite at the Tanglewood, he's not too well. But he's a Sun-squirrel now, would you believe; *and* so are those other two old puffers. Tumbleweed and I have been doing a bit of teaching ourselves since you all left. Shall I give the three old Lords your regards?"

Chapter 32

Rowan returned to his drey after a day's teaching. Meadowsweet was waiting for him. As they brushed whiskers, he said, "You know young Elm Larchson?"

Meadowsweet nodded.

"Today I said to him, 'I didn't see you at the Camouflage and Concealment class yesterday.' And he said, 'Getting good, aren't I?' Cheeky young thing!"

Queen Marguerite had now learned from Wood Anemone how the old King had ordered all the zervantz to eat one of the tiny mushrooms that grew on Old Wally's wall on the night of each new moon, but had never told them why. It had been Wood Anemone, the Royal's zervant Woodlouse as she had been then, who had always maintained a stock of dried mushrooms from The Wall for the ceremonies. When the King had decided that it was necessary for some new zervantz to be born, he had ordered Woodlouse to give different mushrooms to the selected couples instead. This was the secret that she had been sworn to keep.

"We must *educate* all the squirrels so that they know that if they eat Moon Mushrooms each month once they have had two dreylings we can prevent the island from becoming over-populated," Marguerite told Wood Anemone. "That will be your job. No secrets, no coercion, just *education*."

The swan on the beach was ailing and Marguerite did not know what more she could do to help it recover. Then, early in the morning of the day before the New Moon was due, as a light autumn mist floated through the trees of the island, she was trying to get the swan to feed when she sensed that the dolphins were close. She turned and, through the mist, saw three dark humps rise out of the water and disappear again.

"Malin, Lundy, Finisterre," she called, "I am here."

The answer came immediately. "Squirrel-Friend, we see you. Is that a swan with you?"

"Yes, it is covered with black stuff and very sick. I don't know how to help it."

"Only humans can. There is a poison that they throw into the sea from their biggest boats. It kills many birds and hurts us if it gets into our breathing holes," Malin said. "You must get the swan to the humans, only they can save it."

"Have you heard anything about your young friends who we took to the Mainland?" Lundy asked. "We are due to bring them back at first light tomorrow."

"No, I hope they are safe."

"Try and get that swan to the humans, we will see you in the morning."

"SWAN —

WALK ALONG THE BEACH —

220

ACTION NOW —

ACTION NOW!

Yes you can, yes you can,

ACTION NOW — "

The swan responded by raising its head but seemed unable to walk. It was obviously just too sick.

Marguerite left it and went inland, looking for a human. She found one just taking off his green covering with the badge of Acorn, the first squirrel in the World. Underneath was another covering which was white with dark lines making squares on it. As she hid and watched, the human fumbled with his square-patterned arm coverings and rolled them up towards his shoulders. Then he picked up a stick with a flat bit of metal on one end and swung it at the trunk of a rhododendron bush. The top of the bush fell off and rolled towards Marguerite who crouched in fear.

Eventually she collected enough courage to hop out towards the man and chatter to attract his attention. He stopped chopping and leant on the axe-handle watching the squirrel. She ran backwards trying to get him to follow her but he did not move. She tried again and again until it seemed that at last he understood. He rested the axe against a bush, picked up his green covering and followed her.

Marguerite stayed on the ground, looking back frequently to see that she was still being followed, but staying far enough in front to be able to leap clear if the human tried to do anything hostile or unexpected.

She led him to the swan, who hissed feebly. The man approached it cautiously then tied a knot in the end of one of the arm tubes on the green covering he was carrying. He manoeuvred the swan's head into that tube and pulled the rest of his covering over the swan's body so that it could not struggle nor peck him. Marguerite admired the firm but gentle way he had done this and, as he lifted the swan, she slipped away into the shoreline vegetation. The swan was now the human's responsibility. She had done all *she* could. She felt tired and hungry and spent the remainder of that day resting or feeding listlessly, and the night sleeping alone in a palm tree in the valley.

Next morning she hurried through the mist across the island to Pottery Point and joined a group of other squirrels as they watched the three dolphins carrying the sticks and the five returning scouts. Five?

Burdock the News-squirrel carried the story across the island, bearing in mind what her mother, Queen Marguerite, had told her.

"From now on, you will be as responsible as the Post-squirrels were. What you say must be the truth, and if you don't know the truth, find out before you say a word to any squirrel."

SCOUTING PARTY RETURNS.
ROSEBAY GIVES HER LIFE TO SAVE
HER SISTER
With the return of the scouting party your reporter learned of the sad death of Rosebay Wood Anemone's daughter . . .

Chip had been the last one to come ashore; swimming with the coin in his mouth. He had helped Willowherb up the beach but then had avoided the group clustered around the other scouts and had carried the golden disc away to his drey. Later he learned from Burdock that Marguerite was now Queen of Ourland.

He waited until he found her alone.

"I've brought you a present," he said. "A present fit for a Queen."

Marguerite took the coin and turned it over. She had not looked at it closely before.

"It's very pretty," she said as the sun glowed on the bright golden metal. "What's it for?"

"It's for you," Chip replied.

"I didn't mean that, Chip-Friend. What does a squirrel use it for?"

"I don't know," Chip admitted. "But Lundy said that the humans think highly of these. There's a little human's head on one side."

"Then I think we'd better give it back to the humans, don't you? It really belongs to them. But thank you for bringing it to show me."

Chip carried his coin through the wood, unsure how to get it to a human. Although none had ever harmed him, he did not know if it was safe to approach one.

He passed many squirrels busy with harvesting the plentiful nuts. Soon it will be our Harvest Sun-day, he thought, as Willowherb, sitting close to her mother, Wood Anemone, waved to him, a ripe hazel nut in her teeth. He had not noticed before what a good looking squirrel she was.

Ahead, the late morning Sun shone on the tower of the

little island church of St Mary, Brownsea. Chip saw this and was drawn in that direction. As he neared the building he could hear the singing of the humans and he hid behind a slab of stone until they all came out.

He was too afraid of such tall creatures to approach closely and so stayed hidden until he was sure that they had gone. The flat wood that the humans used to close the entrance to this great Man-drey was not across the opening, and he was tempted to enter the dark entrance. As he stood timorously in the doorway waiting for his eyes to adjust to the fainter light, he could smell the scent of fruit and newly dug vegetables of every kind. Around him a harvest of human food was piled in heaps on every ledge and in baskets on the floor.

Where could he put his coin so that a human would find it?

He hopped onto a seat and then onto a ledge higher up; he could leave it there. Then, overwhelmed by an urge to hide it out of sight, he frantically looked around for a suitable place to conceal the coin. A closed wooden box at his paw had a slot in it of just the right size. He looked around the church, fearful of being found, rubbed the coin with his paw one last time, enjoying the smooth feel of it, then dropped it through the slot. As he hopped down from the seat he heard it fall with a rattle into the box, on the side of which in human symbols meaningless to him were the words:

FOR THE POOR AND HUNGRY
PEOPLE OF THE WORLD.

Chapter 33

Chip felt strangely relieved as he left the church. He felt too, that he ought to tell Marguerite what he had done and went to find her.

She was sleeping in the warm afternoon sunlight on a branch outside her drey. He sat and watched her lovingly until she awoke. There was something that he wanted to ask her.

"Marguerite-Friend," he began, then paused, embarrassed. Could he address her as intimately as this, now she was Queen?

She looked at the younger squirrel and remembered how he had looked when she first had seen him, an under-fed and sorry looking sqrunt. He had certainly come up in the trees since then.

"Yes?" she said kindly.

"I was – I was going to ask you – ask you . . ." He stopped again.

"Yes, Chip-Friend?"

"I was going to ask you to be my life-mate – but now that you're Queen . . ."

"That would have made no difference if it had been the

right thing to do," she said. "But it would not be fair. I've had two dreylings and you haven't had any. If I'm going to ask all other squirrels to have only two, then *I* mustn't have any more. You must find another mate. But thank you – I do appreciate the compliment."

Marguerite brushed whiskers with him.

"Now go and visit Wood Anemone, there is someone there who needs you."

Chip hopped away, once again surprisingly light-hearted. He found Wood Anemone with Willowherb, both spreading out Moon Mushrooms to dry in the sun, and he watched them from a distance. The sunlight was lighting up Willowherb's ruddy fur and shining through the glossy hairs of her tail. He knew what he should do.

He went across the grass to her side.

"Willowherb-Friend. Will you be my life-mate?"

"Yewr life-mate uz *will* be."

Chipling brushed whiskers with Willowherb, then with Wood Anemone, who appeared to be as pleased as her daughter who was already racing up a tree, giving a tease-call for him to follow her.

Winter passed, with all of the squirrels who had already had two or more dreylings happily joining in the monthly Moon Mushroom Eating ceremonies. March came in gently to the peaceful island.

Marguerite was on her way to choose which of the newly qualified scouts would be selected to be taken, by the dolphins, for the next Mainland Adventure. Hearing the W-wow-W-wow-W-wow of wing-beats overhead, she looked up as a swan, its feathers gleaming white, swept overhead and turned in a long glide to land in the lagoon and paddle over to where she sat near the edge of the black mud of the Zwamp. The bird was carrying a plant in its beak.

It walked up to her, spread its wings and lowered its head in an unmistakable gesture of thanks, then walked to the marsh-edge and pushed the roots of the plant into the mud where the stream ran into the lagoon, above the level of the highest flood-tide. It lowered its head once again, then walked back into the water.

Marguerite waited as it ran across the surface and lifted into the air. She watched it circle above her and fly westwards, the sound of its wing-beats fading into the distance. Only then did she hop over to look at the plant the swan had brought; it was not familiar to her. It had glossy green leaves and hard round buds, one of which showed a trace of yellow where the sepals were just beginning to open.

Each day she made a point of visiting the marsh, and on the day when the humans were celebrating *their* Spring Sunday, Marguerite found the gift-plant covered in a mass of gleaming golden flowers, brighter and more beautiful by far than the metal disc that Chip had spent so much effort in bringing to Ourland.

She would declare *this* day to be the squirrels' Spring Sun-day too. She went to find Burdock, the News-squirrel; her daughter would enjoy spreading the word.

As she passed The Wall the sound of happy young squirrel voices reached her ears. Marguerite climbed the crumbling brickwork until she could see, at the far end, her grandson Hickory, son of her son Oak and his life-mate Bluebell. Young Hickory was playing the part of Leaper in the Wall game. He saw Marguerite and waved a paw, then greeted her shyly.

"Hello, Marguerite-Ma-Ma." Then he turned away and started the chant:

> *I honour birch-bark*
> *The Island Screen. Flies stinging*
> *A piece of the sun.*

Marguerite smiled to herself. Some things never change, she thought.